TWISTED FATES

TALES FROM THE TAROT

ADAM J. RIDLEY

Cover art: Fae Quin
Cover design: Amanda Meuwissen
Book layout: Amanda Meuwissen
Editor: Jo Bird
Line/Copy Editor: Barb Toth

Printed in the United States of America

X

PROLOGUE

IT HAD BEEN MANY years since the old wizard had heard the call. He paused to catch his breath before stepping through the door. The Magic Shop tended to show up when or where needed, and despite the internal call, Elias had struggled to find the location, proof his powers had begun to wane.

His replacement should've materialized decades before, and the world was lucky something catastrophic hadn't happened with the Legacy Wizard's powers diminishing. He knew that would change soon enough. It always did.

The warmth hit him as he walked into the shop. Smiling, he took in his familiar surroundings, where few things had changed since last he stepped in here, twenty, maybe thirty years earlier. His thick, bushy eyebrow rose when he saw the coffee station tucked into a corner, and he glanced around to see if maybe the old man had finally taken an apprentice.

Unlikely, the wizard thought, *I'd be more likely to sprout a new head.*

"Elias, so good to see you," The Owner said.

The wizard peered through his bushy eyebrows and smiled at his old friend. "I'm not sure I had a choice," he said, but his tone betrayed him, and the bite of his words fell flat. He truly was pleased to see the ageless man.

"Shall we get started then?" The Owner asked.

Elias nodded and, using his cane, followed him through the store to a corner where he did his readings.

It had been well over a hundred years when Elias had first come into this very store, sat in this same chair, and had his cards read. He'd been a young man, too young to drive had he been one of today's youngsters.

"Youngest Wizard in over a thousand years," The Owner had said, and Elias chuckled at the memory. To this day, he still didn't know The Owner's name. As far as he knew, no one did.

The Owner shuffled the cards, stopped, looked up at Elias, then shuffled again. "I wondered if the cards would ever call you, Elias, and even now, they hesitate to speak to your future."

Elias laughed quietly to himself before responding. "The cards or the dealer?"

He smiled and laid a card face down, speaking as only one card was laid. "The past, the present, the future."

It was unusual for him to pull only a single card, but one didn't question a master. Certainly not this master.

He laid the rest of the cards beside him and flipped the one he'd pulled from the deck.

Death stared back at Elias, then he laughed out loud before that turned into a coughing fit. When he recovered, he put his hand on the table next to the card. "Did I need to drag myself out into the winter weather for you to show me this?" Elias asked and chuckled again. "I'm older than any man alive. I only live because my successor has yet to come forward. Of course, death awaits me."

The Owner didn't respond. Instead, he moved Death to the left. Elias shouldn't have been surprised to see another card below it. The old magician had always loved a dramatic moment, and Elias was long past being surprised at his showmanship.

When he flipped the card over, the Fool stared up at them, and Elias smiled. "So, he finally comes?" he asked, and the man across from him nodded.

When Elias looked back at the Fool card, it had magically changed, and in its place was the Wheel of Fortune. "The wheel is turning for you, Elias. Death will not wait much longer. Are you ready to pass the mantle?"

The magician held his hand out, and Elias took it. "It's a relief, and it should've been passed long before now."

Elias lifted his cane and tapped the top. A small chamber opened, and a beautiful white gold ring stared up at him, the bright red ruby shining from its hiding place. "No other may hold the ring except the reader of the cards. And only then to transfer the power."

"It is time," the magician said.

Elias removed the ring from the cane. It had been decades since he'd been able to wear it, his fingers too gnarled from years of performing his duties. Years of wars with the dark forces who would even now gladly destroy the universe and everything in it.

Elias didn't blink, didn't hesitate. He'd been waiting for this moment when the transfer would occur. He took the ring in his hand and gave it to the magician.

"My will is made up. The one who follows me won't have to fight to survive as I did. He will inherit all that I've owned. My attorneys will see to it. He must simply show them the ring. They will do the rest."

The magician smiled. "Come, my old friend, a car waits for you outside."

Elias paused at the door, drawing his old friend and ally into a final embrace. The ring had been handed over as it had for Legacy Wizards throughout the millennia. His life, if he was lucky, would end before the following day. This would be the last time he would be here in The Magic Shop with his beloved friend.

"Safe travels, brother," The Owner whispered.

Elias nodded and left. He felt the wave of air flow as the shop disappeared behind him—another dramatic flair, of course. Elias stepped forward and crawled into the car, its back door open.

"May the successor have an easier time than I," he said, and the door closed beside him. The turning of the Wheel of Fortune was meant to create strife. Through adversity came growth, but the new Legacy Wizard did not need to suffer as he had.

The car moved forward, and Elias leaned his head back against the luxurious leather seat. He had done all he could for his successor, whoever it would be. He just hoped it was enough because the Death card hardly played fair.

Sure, it probably meant he was dying, but it most assuredly had another meaning as well. The world would need the new wizard sooner rather than later. Things were changing. Energy had begun to flow in a different direction.

May the gods help the new wizard because whoever they were, they would need it.

CHAPTER ONE

DAMIAN

I SAT STUCK IN traffic again—unfortunately, a product of my job. Luckily, my passenger didn't mind a little music and even asked me to turn the sound up when Jim Morrison began to play. They were my dad's favorite songs, and after he passed, I transferred his playlist over to my own.

Traffic was always backed up on I-5, but today was worse. I glanced in the mirror, and the woman I'd picked up thirty minutes ago didn't appear disturbed. Unfortunately, the longer the journey took, the less money I'd be making.

"I'm going to try a back route. It normally takes longer, but there must be a few wrecks ahead of us, so it'll be faster than just sitting here."

The woman didn't glance up, just waved her hand, indicating she didn't mind the route change. It took another five minutes to get over to the exit lane and another ten to reach the exit. Luckily, no one else seemed to be taking this exit.

They didn't know the secret of going through Anderson's parking lot to get to one of the outer roads. I thanked my father, who'd driven a cab in Seattle for forty years, for that valuable little secret.

I kept my eye on the passenger as I navigated around the back parking lots and eventually onto the road that skirted the downtown area, taking me to the neighborhood where I was supposed to have dropped my passenger off by now.

Nothing bothered her, so I kept my mouth shut and navigated the busy side streets until I got to the Queen Anne neighborhood. When I hit a heavy patch of fog, I slowed down and once again glanced in the mirror to make sure my passenger wasn't freaking out. Tourists were sometimes surprised at how quickly a fog could settle in this close to the water.

The woman was still focused on her phone, so if she was a tourist, she didn't seem overly concerned. As the fog grew thicker, I began to worry. I couldn't remember the last time it'd been this thick. We always tended to have a little fog this time of year, but this was next level.

I probably should've pulled over, but I was just a block away from my destination, so I risked it, driving slowly through the streets, which luckily were empty. My phone announced I'd arrived at my destination, and I quickly sighed.

"I think we finally made it..." I stopped short when I turned around and saw the woman was gone, like, totally gone.

When had she gotten out of the car? I shook my head. *Passengers*. I found a safe place to park and pulled in, afraid someone would rear-end me if I remained in the street. I also did not want to move on until some of this fog cleared, which would happen when we began to get a little rain.

I'd been a hired driver for five years now. Dad had wanted me to work for his taxi company, but to be honest, I liked my company's policy of letting me drive my own car. It also afforded me a little more freedom. I loved that I could pick someone up, and all the financials were handled for me. Dad's taxi company had begun switching to similar programs, but my company was still more efficient.

After sitting in the car for a few moments, I got a ding on my phone, telling me I'd gotten an excellent rating from the woman who'd disappeared. "That's good, at least," I said out loud and smiled at the nice tip she'd also left. The tip was good enough to forgo another passenger for an hour if I had to.

I logged out of the system and decided to find a nice coffee shop. The fog was beginning to seep into my bones, even if it was outside the car. There's a reason why we Seattle folks liked our coffee so much.

If anything, the fog seemed to thicken as I stepped out into it. What the heck was going on? I wondered as I crossed in front of my car, heading down the sidewalk. I pondered how strange the fog made everything look, almost as if I'd stepped back in time. I couldn't see the cars parked along the street and could barely make out the stores. Unfortunately, they all appeared to be closed as well.

I finally came to a small place that sat squatly between two larger buildings. I couldn't be entirely sure, though, with fog this thick. I could barely make out the words Magic Shop and only because they were a bright red script on a white background.

I almost walked by because the last thing I needed was a felt top hat or a wand that threw out fake flowers, but just as I was about to walk past the door, a loud roar echoed around me. Now, clearly, it was a stupid foghorn, but damn, in this fog it sounded ominous.

Almost instinctively, I reached for the shop's door and sighed in relief as the knob turned in my hand, showing it was open. I quickly scurried in, shutting the door behind me.

I looked up, scanning the interior. I'm not sure I'd have called it a magic shop. That wasn't what this seemed to be at all. Instead, it looked more like somewhere you got your palm read or bought crystals to keep negative spirits away.

I immediately felt safe and warm, though, and having just faced what was clearly an unreasonable fear of fog, especially in the freaking city of fog, I happily began exploring.

The shelves were typical for an older bookstore. There was ample dust, but in a comforting, "this is a real bookstore" kind of way.

The aisles were narrow, but even that felt comforting. I chuckled when I saw the quintessential rack of crystals. My heart leaped when I saw the coffee counter. I didn't hesitate to rush over, then realized the damn thing was closed and from the look of it had been for some time. "Damn," I said.

"Careful what you're damning, young wizard," a voice came from behind me. I turned and saw a handsome older man with a sly smile.

"Um, sorry, I-I just wanted some coffee."

The man didn't move or respond. Instead, he stared for a long moment as if assessing me. "Come with me," he finally said, and like a fool, I did. In my defense, I thought he might have some coffee brewed in a back room or something and empathized with my need for caffeine.

I sighed audibly when the man sat behind what appeared to be a card table, like my great granny used to use when her friends came over to play gin rummy. It was covered with a black velvet cloth, and next to it was a gigantic crystal ball. *Here we go,* I thought.

I was just about to open my mouth to tell the guy I didn't believe in hocus pocus, but he waved his hands, and a deck of cards appeared. "Okay, that's cool. What else you got?" I asked sarcastically.

The man smiled and spread the cards out. I hadn't noticed until now they were Tarot cards, probably because the last two guys I dated professed to be fortune tellers, and neither could tell what we were going to have for supper, much less the future beyond that.

"Sometimes, your skepticism can block your ability to see," the man said as if he could read my thoughts.

"Sometimes it keeps you from being taken advantage of as well," I countered, and the man chuckled, smiling at me like an adult at a petulant child. I thought about leaving, but the fog was too thick, and I liked the store, even if it was full of ridiculous magical stuff I didn't believe in.

"Tell me, young Damian, what causes such a powerful wizard to second-guess the mysteries of our world?"

I laughed before shaking my head. "Okay, you're good. I have no idea how you know my name, but I'm no wizard, witch, werewolf, or other. Why don't you show me how you do the card trick, and I'll buy a deck of cards for my friend who keeps fixing me up with guys who think they can use them?"

Ignoring me now, the man began to shuffle the cards, and I had to give him credit for handling my attitude as well as he was. Molly's friends hated me and had no problem telling me to my face. Of course, I'd dated and dumped two of those friends, but they *had* been cheating, lying assholes.

"The darkness gathers, young wizard," he said, and I smiled, thinking that would be the perfect line for a new video game. "The transfer of power from one powerful mage to another always comes with risk. Pick a card, but let your instinct guide you. Let your future be known through the cards."

I didn't resist the urge to roll my eyes, but why the hell not? It's not like I hadn't done all this before. I ignored the "look inside yourself" nonsense and took the first card my hand landed on. I tried to pull it out, but it felt stuck in concrete.

The man's eyes didn't leave mine. "Pick the card your heart tells you to pick, not the first one you come to."

I tried another card, and it too was stuck. "How are you doing that?" I asked, thinking I really did need to bring Molly here to try the place out.

"Try again. This time, focus on the cards. Which one *feels* like the one for you?"

I don't know why. Maybe it was the fog, maybe the cute shop, or maybe it was because I knew Molly would freak out when I brought her here, but I did as he asked and focused on the cards. For a brief second, one card seemed to glow. I reached out and took it. This time, it came free.

I flipped it over and saw the Wheel of Fortune. "Ah, you've come to a crossroads. Darkness has played in your life," he said, pointing toward the weird drawing of a snake on the left side of the card. "But Hermes, shown here as Anubis, guides your future. Are you ready to accept your gifts? Are you ready to take up the mantle, young wizard?" he asked, and I almost laughed.

Before I could say something sarcastic, the world went dark, and I couldn't see anything, like nothing. I would've jumped up and searched for my phone, something to give light, but I couldn't move. *What's going on?* I wanted to yell, but I couldn't even do that.

"The darkness is here. It seeks to stop you from taking your position. Fight it, push it away," a voice said in my head.

"How?" I asked, freaking out but still unable to speak out loud.

"Trust your instincts. Trust your own powers," the voice replied.

I forced myself to focus on my core, as Molly had told me when she'd tried teaching me some magic thing or another. I felt warmth spread and flow from my abdominal area, and fill my body. I immediately got movement back and, instinctively, I threw my hands out. Light erupted from them, from me, filling the shop.

The man across from me looked as if he'd passed out, and I quickly rushed over to him. "Hey, mister, are you okay?"

He slowly came to and nodded. "You've passed the test. Now you've also had a taste of what you'll have to face."

Slowly, he sat up and gestured for me to sit back down. "I can't advise you much. I can only read the cards, but I can give you this," he said, unclenching his fist, and a beautiful ring appeared there as if by magic.

"What's this?" I asked.

"Something that now belongs to you. Can you try it on?"

I was mesmerized by the ring, my entire body throbbing with the need to take it from him, but something held me back, something primal.

I ignored the warning, letting my desire to hold the ring overcome the fear, and immediately slipped it onto my finger.

"The mantle has been passed," the man said, and I felt dizzy at the proclamation.

Once again, my world darkened, but unlike a moment ago, this felt intentional, like my own doing. I saw the image of a man. He was slight of build, dark complected, dark hair. At first, I wondered if he and the man across from me were related, but no. I somehow knew he wasn't.

When the image cleared, the man who'd been standing across from me now stood at the front door. "What the hell?" I asked, and the man put his finger up.

"Careful, you are a powerful wizard. Words have consequences." I wanted to chuckle, but weird things were happening. "Follow your instincts, young man. Go where they lead," he said and handed me a card. "Your predecessor wanted you to go here. He didn't want you to start your journey with no resources. They should be able to help."

I took the card and looked at it. Stages, and Harrison, Attorneys at Law, the card read. "Okay," I said, but when I glanced up, I was no longer in the shop. I was standing on the sidewalk in front of... Shit, this would be funny if it wasn't freaky. I was standing in front of a coffee shop where the weird magic shop had been. Oh, and there was no fog in sight.

Chapter Two

OWEN

I stared out the huge plate glass window as the rain descended over the Puget Sound. I loved Seattle. Well, I mostly loved it. I was getting more than a little tired of the rain and lack of sunshine, but the town was always happening. It always had a little magic in the air.

My bosses, the firm's two partners, had just left for the day, and I was stuck here doing a glorified paralegal's work. Not that I minded. I had worked for my mom's firm back in Illinois before moving out here, and I had been her legal assistant. Of course, she also made me part janitor, part investigator, and, well, anything that needed doing.

Foolish of me. I had thought when I got my law degree and passed all the stupid exams, I'd be doing lawyer work. At least the two older partners here weren't insane about logging every damned second to bill clients. Of course, that's why I decided to apply to small firms. I couldn't see myself chasing every penny.

I sighed, let out a heavy, labored breath, and returned to the piles of paperwork. I didn't hear the door open and almost missed Cary's breathless call. "You won't believe this," he said, pulling me out of the chair.

"Believe what? Cary, what's going on?" I asked.

"Do you remember that old man that came in with the weird will? The one that gave all his money and possessions to 'the one who bears the ring'?" he asked, changing his voice to sound like someone from *The Lord of the Rings* or something.

I laughed. "No, and that sounds ridiculous. Cary, I have like fifty hours' worth of work to do here. Go screw with Mrs. Patterson," I said, referring to our one very beleaguered and elderly legal assistant.

"You're the only attorney in, so you've got to see him. Come on, he's hot, too, really hot!" Cary said, pulling me down the hallway.

I just shook my head and accepted that I wouldn't get anything done until Cary got his way. As the front desk clerk, he was usually solid as a rock, but when he lost his mind, usually over some hot guy, he lost it entirely.

I stepped into the lobby and froze. Six three, maybe six four? I couldn't quite tell with his long coat, but he was tall, just like I liked my men.

Dark, almost coal-black hair and bright blue eyes—such a weird contrast against his pale skin. I'd swear he was almost some kind of vampire with features like that. "Hi, I'm...I'm

Damian Richards. I-I was given this card and told to show you my ring?"

He blushed, and honestly, that just made him that much more attractive, making his previous unapproachable appearance seem a bit more, well, approachable.

"I-I, um, I don't know what that means," I said, and Cary, who'd disappeared, came back and shoved a file in my hands, then pushed me toward the conference room, all while making eyes at the handsome stranger.

"O-okay," I stuttered. "Um, come in, and I'll review the file."

The man seemed as confused as me, which helped, I guess. I walked into the conference room and grabbed him a bottle of water, not thinking to ask if he wanted one. I needed something, so I grabbed two as I figured we could both use one.

I took a long swig before sitting next to him. "I apologize. I'm not up on your case, so give me a minute to read the file," I said, wishing he'd shown up thirty minutes earlier so he could have met with one of the partners who at least might have understood what was happening.

I scanned the file, then, perplexed, scanned it again. The list of assets was significant. A home in the affluent Queen Anne neighborhood that even I, new to Seattle, knew was worth a lot. There was also well over six million dollars, among other things, some of which sounded like they had come from a fairy tale.

But that wasn't the perplexing part. What I didn't understand was the ring. "He who wears the ring—" The file showed several pictures of it, all from different angles. "—shall inherit all my assets."

"You, um, have the ring?" I asked.

He placed his hand on the table, the ring almost glowing. It was beautiful, probably worth thousands, if not tens of thousands, of dollars. "Um, can I take a closer look?" I asked.

He shook his head. "No, I-I can't get it off."

"Oh, well, okay, let me see your hand, then," I said, more because I didn't know what the fuck else to do. He held his hand out, and I stared at it briefly. His hand was bigger than mine, and I didn't have little hands.

He was a large but well-built man, and his hands were the same. "Okay," I said, reaching out and taking his fingers.

I was momentarily blinded, like someone had turned the lights out. By the time the light returned, the guy was holding my hand, his eyes the size of saucers. "You," he said. "I-I saw you."

"You did? Where?" I asked, confused and still lightheaded from whatever episode I'd just had.

"This...this is too weird. I-I'm going to go."

I stood as he did, and just as he was about to leave, the ring began to glow for real, and it wasn't my imagination. "Take what I've left you," a disembodied voice said, and I immediately felt clammy, like when I had a virus and stood up too fast.

I sat back down, my stomach doing flip-flops, and when I looked up, the guy had done the same. "What's going on?" I asked.

The guy shook his head. "I'm... I don't know. Something weird."

I nodded. "You can say that again. Did your ring just talk?" I asked.

He shrugged. "Apparently. I don't know, I literally just got the thing."

"Maybe you should take it back."

"I get the feeling," he said, staring down at the ring in front of him, "it's not going to be that easy."

CHAPTER THREE

DAMIAN

I T HAD BEEN A weird-ass day—from the moment the fog appeared, the woman in my car disappearing, the strange store with the weird guy reading cards, and not to mention getting the ring. Now, here I sat in a lawyer's office, which I tended to avoid if possible. Lawyers were nothing but trouble. Advice my dad gave me, and I'd always considered useful.

The problem was I'd seen a vision of this particular lawyer in the weird magic shop. I hadn't recognized him until he took my hand, but now I knew it was definitely the same guy.

"So," he finally said after we stared at each other for a moment. "I, um, I'm going to read you the will, like you know, that's what we do," he added, but I could tell he was as nervous as me.

I listened as he read the will, and my eyes bugged when he listed the assets. "No way," I said. "This is a joke, some kind of weird prank, right?"

He shook his head and shrugged. "I'm going to have Cary call the partners. I'm sorry, I don't quite understand."

I nodded and read the will again after the guy, Owen, I think his name was, handed it over, then got up to talk to the little twink who'd met me when I first came in. He was on the phone with someone for several minutes before he came back, his face flushed. "Okay, so I just talked to my boss. The will is legal, I guess, but we have some forms you have to sign," he said, fumbling through the folder until he came to a bunch of papers held together with a paper clip.

He quickly read them and handed them to me to sign. "I need to see your license. The partners want me to put a copy in your file. You need to fill these out, then it's all yours."

"This is crazy. I didn't even know this guy."

"Listen, this isn't a small amount of money or assets. I'd sign while you can. I'll work with my boss tomorrow and figure out anything we might've missed, but you should jump on this now," he said.

I couldn't disagree. It was a dream come true, even if it was really weird. I gave him my license and read and signed the forms making me a fucking millionaire. *Surely, it wouldn't be this easy,* I thought. The other shoe would drop, but at least it was a fun dream. Even if I ended up on some reality TV show, maybe they'd pay me for that. Millions of dollars? Probably not, but at least it might be enough that I could stop driving passengers as much and maybe finish my degree.

Owen returned a few moments later, talking on his phone. "Yes, sir, of course, yes, I can do that. I don't need to do anything else, maybe before..." He paused and looked at me, confusion crossing his face, but he nodded. "Okay, just take him to the house and give him the key that's in the file. Yes, you want me to escort him there, okay. Yes, I... Yes, sir, I can do that too."

He hung up and shook his head. "This has been by far the strangest thing I've ever been through, and I worked for my mother five years while going to law school." He took the documents I'd signed, examined them, made me initial something I'd missed, and then took the forms to the guy Cary, who made copies. "The partners want me to escort you to your new home. You'll need to come back tomorrow so they can help you make all the right moves to keep the Internal Revenue Service happy, but according to them, it's all yours now."

Cary came back smiling and even winked at me, which was almost the straw that broke the camel's back. But he disappeared again fast enough, thank goodness. "Okay, well, here's the address. I'm afraid I'll have to take a ride service over. Did you drive?" he asked.

Just then, my phone dinged, and I knew even before I checked that I was his ride. I'd turned the damned service off. I knew that for a fact, and had I not, I would've gotten several calls to drive at this time of day in downtown Seattle, especially with the weather turning bad.

I laughed when I saw I was supposed to pick him up. Okay, more weird, way too much weird in one day. I turned my phone to show him. "I am a professional driver, and just so you know, that was turned off. Apparently, someone wants me to drive you there."

He shook his head and studied me a long time before sighing. "If you kill me, Cary has seen your face, and we have your license on file. So, this better not be some weird murder thing."

I laughed. "Some weird murder thing? I think you've been watching too much true crime."

The guy chuckled. "New town, new life, I admit it. TV is my boyfriend at the moment."

Did he just tell me he's gay? Of course, if this wasn't a reality TV show, and some guy didn't pop out to tell me it had been a hoax, I had just become a millionaire. I was now prime real estate.

I'll admit Owen didn't seem like the type to care that much. You could always tell the players; at least, I could after driving professionally all these years, and before that, riding in the taxi with my dad. People were usually easy to read, and this guy seemed like one of the good ones.

Of course, I could be high on something, and this was all just some hallucination. Either way, I'd be storing this guy's number in my phone. Something I never did, but on this occasion, I was going to make an exception.

Chapter Four

OWEN

Bizarre. So freaking bizarre. I grabbed the keys that were in the folder before I followed the guy out of the office to his Honda Accord. Sure enough, he had the company's logo on the side, telling me he was at least legit.

I almost got in the back since the situation was a little freaky, but I forced myself to get over it and ride up front with him, especially since he was one of our wealthiest clients now. I should at least try to make a good impression.

"So, you drive professionally, and now you're a millionaire?" I asked, then cringed. "Sorry, don't answer that. I shouldn't have asked."

He laughed. "You've about summed it up. I'm waiting for the reality TV guy to pop out of the woodwork to tell me this has all been a hoax."

"It'll be on both of us, then. I mean, I didn't even know you could pass all your worldly possessions to someone who owned a ring."

Damian chuckled. "I didn't either. I...well, I had a strange experience this morning, so I could also be losing my mind or having some bizarre drug trip. I've not quite figured out what's true."

"If you're high, you probably shouldn't be driving."

"If my app hadn't turned back on by itself, I wouldn't be."

"Yeah," I said and laughed. "Okay, so it's bizarre for both of us."

Conversation stalled as he navigated the busy side streets between the office and his new home. He pulled up in front of a gigantic Victorian house, and both of us just stared at it. "Um, this is it?" he asked.

I looked at the file and the address, then back at the address on the street. "Yes, I-I think so."

"Okay, you're the attorney. You go first."

I glanced over at him and wanted to argue because the place totally appeared to be haunted, but I couldn't. I represented the firm that represented him. He wasn't wrong. We got out, and I walked toward the iron gate separating the house from the sidewalk, and sure enough, there was a key that fit. I slipped it in and turned.

Nothing happened. "It...it doesn't seem to work," I said.

"Here, can I have a try?" he asked, and I stepped back. When he twisted it, the gate slid open and didn't even squeak.

"That's so strange," I said, but he just shrugged and walked through. When he tried to return the key to me, I lifted my hands. "No, it's yours, clearly," I said, making him laugh.

I didn't even try the front door. Instead, I handed him the other key from his package and let him open it. The giant home and garden television–style wooden door opened just as smoothly for him as the gate had, and I followed him into the house, standing beside him as we gawked.

"This is gorgeous," I said, watching him as he swallowed hard.

"Um, is this really mine?" he asked.

I nodded. "According to the paperwork you just signed, yeah, it is. Okay, well, I'm going to go."

"Oh, hell no," he said and grabbed my arm. "You are so not leaving me alone in a haunted mansion. You're my attorney, right? You gotta stay."

I would've chuckled if he hadn't looked so terrified. "Don't you have a friend you can call?" I asked, and he shook his head.

"Molly, but she's in Portland. Just, you know, stick around while I check it out. I mean, it's creepy, right? It's not just me?"

I took in the foyer. Dark red velvet wallpaper hung from the walls. Old wooden furniture that looked like it'd been here since the house was built gleamed beautifully along the perimeter. An equally beautiful staircase flowed from this floor to what appeared to be a landing above us.

"I mean, it appears old but it's not creepy. It's clean, at least. I have more dust in my apartment, and I've only lived there three months," I said as I observed a beautiful table across from the staircase, an ornate vase sitting on it that showed evidence of years holding fresh flowers.

"Come on," I said, leading him into the room to our right. "My uncle owns a house like this. He and his husband run a bed and breakfast back in my hometown. This should be the parlor or the library," I said, pulling the pocket doors back and leading him inside. "A music room, also pretty classic for the time frame."

I opened another set of pocket doors on a far wall, and sure enough, a library appeared. "This was where the men used to gather back in Victorian times. See." I pointed to the windowsill where someone had burned it with what might have been a cigar.

There was a door leading back to the hallway. "Come back up front because the house was meant to be seen in sections. *This* should be the parlor," I said, opening a door. Sure enough, a beautiful sitting room came into view. I crossed to the fireplace. "Hey, look, the fireplace appears to be still useable. It's really rare to have one of these intact. I'd have it checked out by a chimney sweep though. If it's not been cleaned properly, you could cause a fire."

I was in my element now. I'd loved watching property restoration shows, and all their historic renovations since I was a kid. After my father left, my mom and I would watch the shows to console ourselves. "Ah, as I suspected, here's the dining room. Oh wow, this is spectacular, don't you think? And that chandelier? I bet that's Tiffany glass too. Jeez, this is an amazing place," I said, intrigued by the over-the-top beautiful mansion, and forgetting I was actually with a client.

We walked into a butler's pantry, and I oohed and aahed over all the storage. Then, even though I was expecting it, I cringed when we entered the tiny kitchen. "Yeah, this is typical for older homes. When this was built, only the servants used the kitchens. You could probably have this redone. Now, if I'm not mistaken, this—" I said, leading the way through a small exterior hallway that wound around the back and pointing out a dark room with ugly 1970s paneling, "—is the servant's quarters. Most of the time, servants lived in the basement or top floor, but I'm guessing this one has a ballroom up there instead. Shall we go see?" I turned and saw a very green-looking client who'd followed me through the house. "Oh, wow, sorry. Are you okay?"

He shook his head. "No, no, I'm not. I don't understand any of this. Why would a stranger give this to me? And just because of a ring. Something isn't making sense," he said.

"Hey, come here," I led him back into the kitchen, and we sat at the bar. "Listen, I don't know. I just know this is a real home, and no one lives here, at least not that I can see. Did you notice there are no family photos and no personal items lying around? It's almost as if it was staged for a TV show. Come here," I said, pulling open the drawers on either side of the stove. "There's nothing personal in here either. Follow me." I led him into the dining room and pulled open drawers there as well. "All of it—empty. Someone prepared this for its new owner. I'm guessing it was for you."

"Yeah, but why? Why me?"

"I don't know, but," I said, shrugging, "there's nothing wrong with this house. It's not creepy or haunted, or if it is, no more than any house this age. Come on, let's explore the rest, then you can lock it up until you speak with my bosses tomorrow. I'm sure they'll be able to shed more light on the situation."

Chapter Five

DAMIAN

I FOLLOWED OWEN UP the stairs, and we explored the rooms. They were all decorated in what he called Victorian style. It wasn't ugly, but it was too fussy for me. I was a simple guy who liked simple things, and this was just too much.

Finally, after touring the second floor and seeing Owen, grinning from ear to ear, I realized it really should've been someone like him who inherited the place. We were just about to walk downstairs when a door creaked open on the next landing. "Okay," Owen said, "now, that was creepy."

I nodded. "Shall we go up?" I asked.

He shrugged. "Your house, so you go first!" he said, and I laughed since that's what I'd said to him when we first arrived.

I walked up the narrow stairs, definitely not as ornate as the staircase that led here. When we got to the top, Owen gasped. "My God, this is... It's like a novel."

He wasn't wrong. Each corner of the roof had huge windows. Stained glass surrounded ovals, which let in natural light. I walked to one of the windows and looked out over the Puget Sound. Mt. Rainier stood off to the side. It was as beautiful as that sight ever was. When I looked closer, I noticed the stained glass depicted the scene through the oval window.

I glanced around the room and saw that each window had similar stained-glass scenes, and I assumed each of them depicted the sight through the clear glass. Lake Washington, the Cascade Mountains, and the Olympic Mountain Range. "Wow, this is truly amazing." I said and scanned the room for Owen.

He was staring at the books on a shelf, his hands tucked behind his back, a look of amazement on his face. When I walked toward him, he sighed. "These...these look like they're centuries old. I don't even dare touch them," he said as he gestured toward the ancient-looking books. There were no titles on the spines, and I had to agree they looked pretty old. "It looks like this was originally a ballroom, as I said earlier, but someone turned it into...into this wonderland."

"It's pretty amazing. Hey, I want to take some pictures to send to my friend. Hold on," I said. I pulled my phone out and tried to get a selfie in front of the massive window with Mt. Rainier in it. When I backed up, I accidentally knocked over a vase, which fell to the ground and shattered. I quickly knelt to pick up the shards and cut myself. "Oh, crap, damn."

"Come over here, and let's get it under the water," Owen said, pulling me into the ancient bathroom. The plumbing worked though, and the cool water washed away the blood.

Owen pulled off some toilet paper and wrapped my finger while trying to find a bandage. "Come on, let's go downstairs and see if there are any down there."

He turned off the faucet and was pulling me toward the stairs, when I suddenly froze. "What?" Owen asked, and I pointed at where the vase had fallen.

Somehow, the shards had been swept up. Nothing was out of place. I looked at my finger just to be sure it was still cut, and sure enough, it was still bleeding.

"Um, I-I think I might be ready to go," I said.

"Yeah, yeah, me too," Owen replied, and we both rushed down the stairs and out the front door.

Chapter Six

OWEN

"Damn," Damian said, and that's all it took for me to crack up.

"Oh my God, that was creepy," I replied, and Damian began laughing as well. "Come on, *professional* driver, I'll take you out for a drink. After that experience, I think we deserve it."

Damian chuckled as we rushed out the front gate.

"You need to lock that up, even if it is haunted as fuck," I said as we got to the car.

He nodded, then unlocked the passenger door to let me in. I watched as he locked the gate but didn't go back to the house. Not that I blamed him.

We went to a bar Damian said he liked, which was nice since I hadn't been here long enough to find anywhere special.

The bar was in a one-story building that looked much like the ones in the town where I grew up in Illinois. Most buildings had been built in the middle of the last century. It looked pretty seedy, but I knew from experience that often meant a fun place to hang out if you had friends with you. Hopefully, he did, and no one would kill us for stepping on their territory.

We walked in and immediately heard someone shout, "Bitch!"

I looked over to see a voluptuous, red-headed diva plow into Damian. "My God, Molly, you're going to knock me down!" Damian said when the woman let him go.

"I missed your brooding ass way too much," she said, then grabbed his face and pulled him down before laying a kiss right on his lips.

Okay, I totally misread the signals. I'd thought the guy was as gay as me. When Molly glanced over and saw me, she smiled mischievously. "Well, well, who is this?" Her expression reminded me a lot of Angelina Jolie in *Maleficent* when she said almost the same thing.

"This is my attorney, Owen. Owen, this is my best friend, Molly. She just got back in town from vacation. Apparently, she missed me," he said chuckling.

Oh, best friend made more sense, provided my gaydar wasn't broken.

"Attorney? Why do you need an attorney?"

I watched as Damian tried to figure out what to say. "I... I sorta inherited some stuff. It's a long story," he said, and I could tell he wanted to leave it at that.

Molly, however, clearly wasn't one to let things go. She drew us both to the bar, where a group of people ranging from Goth to weird stood. Two men gave me a once-over, then looked at Damian with pure hatred, telling me they were likely exes. What had I gotten into?

"You guys, this is Owen. He's an attorney," Molly said and then all but pushed me into a chair and pulled Damian away from the group.

"What kind of attorney?" a woman dressed all in black with various tattoos and piercings asked.

"Um, I work for a small firm, so I don't have a main focus, but I prefer real estate and corporate work."

"Are you any good?" she asked, and I laughed.

"I'm great for a newbie," I responded.

"Seems like destiny has brought you here to me, so here's my card. I'm looking for someone to help me with my contracts. I'm a singer," she said.

"Oh, um, I didn't grab any cards. Can...can I send you an email tomorrow with my information?"

Someone in the group laughed, and I glanced over. "She'd have dumped you if you'd brought cards," they said when I made eye contact.

The woman beside me all but purred. "I don't like conventional business tactics. Attorneys brandishing cards is a sure sign they aren't for me. You, however, seem perfect."

I swallowed hard, suddenly unsure whether being in the haunted house wasn't better than being here. I was totally out of my element.

"I'll be sure to email you as soon as possible."

She winked at me, then turned and began talking to the others in the group. Luckily, everyone seemed to leave me alone, and when the server came over, I ordered a beer. It's not like I didn't like groups. I did, at least groups of people I knew.

I hadn't anticipated being pulled into a group of people I didn't know, or I would've requested something a bit more neutral. However, if I got a client for the firm, that would definitely work well for me.

Damian and Molly returned shortly, thank goodness, and Damian sat down beside me. "You okay?" he asked quietly.

I nodded. "Yes, um, I might have a new client."

Damian cocked an eyebrow when he looked at the card in my hand. "Wow, that's significant," he said, and the woman, Shadow, whose name was on her card, winked at him.

"Come on, we can sit over there for some privacy," Damian said, and I waved awkwardly to the group, not knowing how else to exit the weird situation.

When we sat down, Damian explained how Shadow was a famous local singer and that several record labels had been courting her for the past year, but she'd refused all of them. "If she offered you her card, she must really like you."

I didn't know how to respond. Honestly, I couldn't imagine how meeting me for the first time, especially with how awkward the entire thing felt, would make anyone want to work with me. *Oh well, I won't kick a gift horse in the mouth.*

"What happened in the house tonight? Is this all real? I mean, cut to the chase, Owen," Damian said.

I shrugged. "I promise I had no idea about any of it, and until you speak to my bosses tomorrow, you won't know the entire story, either, but yes, it appears you've really inherited all of it."

"Molly says this whole inheritance thing feels like bad juju."

I cocked my eyebrow. "Is Molly psychic or something?"

He laughed. "Wannabe, yes."

I just shrugged, not knowing what else to do. "Those windows in the attic room were amazing. I would've liked to have spent more time there had it not been for the vase incident," Damian said, pulling out his phone.

"It was freaky, for sure."

Damian flipped through his photos, and I could see when he settled on one. He instantly gasped and blew it up.

"Shit, did you see this?" he asked, showing me.

A perturbed-looking older man stood behind him in the photo. The picture was clearly snapped right before he backed into the vase. The man looked like an old butler. "This can't be real," I said, but Damian just stared at me. "Okay, tomorrow morning, first thing, we should meet at the office and find out what they know. Then...then we'll work out the details."

CHAPTER SEVEN

DAMIAN

As strange as my day had been, I don't think I'd actually absorbed what was happening until I saw the picture on my phone. I'd been working hard to convince myself it was all just a hoax or my mind was making stuff up to make sense of my circumstances, but then, someone cleaned up the broken vase.

Even the events at the magic store could be explained by sleight of hand, but that picture felt real. The old man was see-through. He also looked very put-upon, like you'd expect a butler to be, especially if he knew I was about to knock over a fancy piece of décor.

I guess if I wanted to, I could explain it away, but it felt more real than the rest of the stuff that'd happened, and it wasn't like I didn't have the gash on my finger to prove it.

Owen left shortly after I showed him the picture. I guess he was as weirded out as I was. Of course, Molly sat across from me the moment he was gone. "So, attorney guy is cute, totally your type."

"What do you think my type is?" I asked and glanced at the two guys I'd gone out with, one dressed Goth, the other covered in piercings and tattoos. Neither looked remotely like the other.

"Smaller than you, shy, easygoing."

I laughed. "Um, have you met Whisper and Peace?" I asked, referring to my exes, who were still leering at me from the table nearby.

Molly laughed. "They were never your type, and we both know it. You like the boy next door."

I shrugged. She wasn't wrong. Not that I'd dated many men who looked that way. My friends had always been in the alternative crowd. Whisper and Peace were more like the guys I'd dated since high school. I sipped my beer and wondered if maybe she was right, and Owen *was* my type.

"Okay, so spill, you said you inherited a bunch of stuff, but not how. What's all this about?" she asked.

I shook my head. "Listen, Molly, I'm not exactly sure. Like I told you before, this was all sprung on me today. I'm still trying to wrap my head around it, but I'm going to talk to Owen's bosses tomorrow. They set up the will and stuff. I should know more then."

"Okay, well, want company? I still have another day off before I go back to work."

I thought about it for a moment before responding. Molly would sensationalize all this and likely cause me to get lost in the magical details of it. Right now, I felt like I needed to keep my head.

"No," I said and sighed. "I think I'd better take this one on by myself, but I did inherit a haunted house, or at least I think I did. Maybe you and the spooky kids want to come check it out with me if indeed it's mine."

Molly's face lit up like I'd just given her a million dollars. "Seriously, a real haunted house?"

I laughed, flipped my phone back on, and showed her the photo. "Is this evidence enough?"

"Shit," Molly said. "Yeah, that's pretty spooky shit."

I laughed as she took my phone and showed it to our friends. As usual, half of them accused me of creating a fake, the other half were ready to go meet the old butler ghost right then. When I finally got my phone back, I headed home for the night.

I walked into my dad's old apartment and sighed. It wasn't much. We'd never had a lot of money, and Dad had sold the tiny home we'd owned after Mom died, because it had cut his income in half.

I'd spent most of my life living in the small two-bedroom apartment, and honestly, I felt at home here. It wasn't the mansion with the magnificent windows and the scary butler ghost, but it'd always been mine. What did that mean? I don't know, but I was looking forward to tomorrow morning when I could get to the bottom of the whole thing.

If I'd actually inherited all this stuff, I could finally quit driving and focus on the things I'd wanted or at least thought I wanted before Dad got sick and I had to take on making money. That night I closed my eyes and dreamed of ghostly servants swarming around me.

In the dream, it felt so natural to have spirits tend to my needs, but when I woke up the next morning, only partially rested, I realized ghosts weren't natural at all. Nothing about my experience yesterday had been.

Chapter Eight

OWEN

I GOT TO WORK early the following day and immediately remembered I'd promised Shadow, the woman I'd met at the bar, that I'd send her my information and my company's introductory email. Knowing she wasn't much for convention, I explained I had to attach the policy because it was required.

My bosses dragged in late to the office, a little after nine, and Cary greeted them as usual with a cup of coffee, drip, of course, just as they liked it. He was such a suck-up. He was also a very sweet man and had gone out of his way to make me feel at home, so suck-up or not, I considered him a friend.

I knocked on Mr. Harrison's door because he was the one who hired me and was a lot more approachable than Mr. Stages.

"Hi, um, sir. I wanted to ask you more about the will I distributed assets for yesterday."

"Aah, yes, Elias Ericson's will. How did that go?" he asked.

"Strangely," I admitted, and Mr. Harrison laughed.

"Yes, I'm sure it was. Mr. Ericson was an eccentric old fella but a good man. Died just a week ago. I believe he was a hundred and fifteen. Before he died, he was still moving around like a man half that age."

I cleared my throat to return Mr. Harrison's attention to me and off the road to memory lane. The firm's partner tended to get lost on a tangent. "Well, the gentleman who inherited the estate, Damian Richards, wanted more information than I could give him. I expect he'll be showing up this morning."

He smiled and nodded. "I'm sure he does want more information. Unfortunately, I'm not sure we can help."

Just then, Mr. Stages came into the hallway. "I forgot to put this in the folder. Mr. Ericson brought it in week before last. You say the heir intends to come in today?" he asked.

I nodded and backed away so Mr. Stages could enter Mr. Harrison's office. "Yes, sir. He said he'd be by first thing this morning."

"Good, good, let me know when he comes in."

Mr. Stages closed the door to Mr. Harrison's office, dismissing me. I would've been offended, but when I was hired, Mr. Harrison had made it clear his law partner wasn't good with social convention. He was one of the city's top tax attorneys though. I guess if you aren't good with people, tax law is the best option.

I returned to my office to push the piles of paper around a little more, when Cary came to my office door. "He's here," he said breathlessly.

I chuckled. "Stop perving on the clients," I said. Cary quickly looked around to ensure it was just us, then flipped me off.

I laughed like I usually did at Cary's shenanigans. "Show him into the conference room. I'll get the partners."

"No worries, I already let the partners know Damian was here," he said, disappearing out the door. When I walked into the conference room, I smiled because now that all this business wasn't on my shoulders, I felt more relaxed. "How are you? Feeling better this morning?" I asked.

Damian shook his head. "No, I had weird dreams all night. That butler ghost scared me more than I thought."

"It was scary. Oh, one of the partners has more information for you. Hopefully that'll help."

Just then, Mr. Harrison entered with Mr. Stages behind him. "Mr. Richards," they both said as they took his hand in turn before gesturing for us all to sit.

"I'm afraid we can't give you much more information," Mr. Harrison said immediately, "than what you received yesterday. All we can share is that Elias Ericson made it clear how his estate was to be distributed. When you appeared with the ring, the process was set into motion."

"So this isn't a joke?"

The older men chuckled. "No, this is certainly not a joke. However, I was told to give you this when you collect the keys from us," Mr. Stages said. "Mr. Ericson made it clear you were to open that on your own. Now, I was instructed to help ensure the Internal Revenue Service doesn't come knocking. Shall we dive into that?" Mr. Stages said, handing Damian the manila envelope.

I didn't stick around for the tax conversation. I had too much to do, but I was intensely intrigued by the envelope's contents. Would that explain why the old man had given everything to a stranger? Or the haunting in the attic?

I didn't know, but it was intriguing enough that I had difficulty focusing on the paperwork from hell. By noon, I was so dug in I'd all but forgotten about Damian and the partners discussing legal stuff in the conference room down the hall.

Luckily, when Cary poked his head in to say Damian had requested to see me before he left, I'd cleared about two-thirds of the paperwork off my desk—not that all of it wouldn't be replaced with another pile by the end of the day.

Secretly, I hoped Shadow would get back to me and that her contract would be lucrative enough for me to graduate from doing legal assistant stuff to actually doing attorney work. I'd checked my email less than an hour ago, though, and she hadn't responded. Who knew, maybe she wouldn't. Our meeting was bizarre, after all.

I went out to meet Damian standing in the lobby talking to Cary. "Hey, you wanted to see me?" I asked.

"Um, yeah, are you going to take a lunch break?"

I looked at my watch and smiled. "Yeah, I can do lunch. Cary, I'll be back in an hour," I said, and the receptionist just smiled and waved me off. He was so going to give me so much shit when I got back.

This time, I chose the little deli down the street from the office. I'd eaten there often enough since I'd gotten my job. I loved their Italian meatball sandwich, but I always made a mess eating it, so I decided to go with something less embarrassing. Damian was ridiculously handsome, after all. If there was a chance...

"So, my treat, now I know this is real. Like, really real," he said, causing me to chuckle.

"What're you going to do? I mean, this is a lot to take in on such short notice."

"Probably figure out how to deal with the ghost first, but then, you know, maybe school?"

"Really? That's cool. What do you want to study?" I asked.

Damian shrugged. "I don't know. I was thinking about being a teacher before my father got sick. Then, I don't know. I talked to some teachers, and they shared how horrible it was, so I'm not sure now. What made you wanna be an attorney?" he asked.

I smiled. "I grew up in a law office, not much different than the one I work in now. My mother is an attorney. Then, she became our circuit judge. I guess it's always just been who I am."

"Wow, your mom is a judge?" he asked.

"*Was*. She's semi-retired now."

"Why don't you work for her?" Damian asked.

I moved the chips around my plate and sighed. "I... I dated a guy. Football player, small-town hero type. Eric Strange was his name. He got his law degree a few years before me, and Mom hired him. He basically took over her firm. Long story short, I found out he was playing me to get a way in. He screwed most of the gay guys in Central Illinois before I finally figured out what was going on."

I stared at my plate for a few moments before I looked up. "I was humiliated, and the saddest part was so was my mother. She threatened to fire him, but to do that would've cost her so much money. The son of a bitch was bringing in so much cash I decided it was best to move on and leave him to it."

"Wow, what did your mother say?" he asked.

I laughed, the bitterness coating the humor, before I could pull it back. "My mother is a pragmatist. When I left, she accepted that as my defeat. I have to admit, though, I got the better end of it. I left the small town on the prairie and now live in one of America's most amazing cities. I don't have to deal with homophobia. In fact, I could lean over the table and kiss you right now, and I doubt anyone would look twice."

When I looked up, Damian was smiling. "Do you want to kiss me?" he asked, and my face instantly flushed bright red.

"I-I didn't mean that."

"I know, but the question still begs to be answered: Do you want to kiss me?"

I swallowed hard but nodded. "I-I wouldn't pass up the chance if you're offering."

Damian leaned his tall body toward me, not even needing to stand to reach. I didn't hesitate. Instead, I leaned forward and took his incredible mouth with mine. He tasted of lunch and something darker, more masculine. I wanted more...wanted so much more, but I suddenly remembered we were in the middle of a public restaurant during the lunch hour.

I pulled back, blushing even deeper. My instinct was to look around to see if anyone had seen us, but with Damian's piercing blue eyes focused on me, I couldn't look away. "So, that was nice," he said.

"Yeah?"

"Yeah. Why don't you have dinner with me tonight? I'd like to do more of the kissing thing, but my friend Molly has already texted me eleven times about going to the house this evening. Wanna join us?"

I nodded. "Yeah, I mean, yes, I'd like to do both, um, you know, the kissing and the ghost hunting."

Damian laughed out loud. "That's totally what they want to do."

I glanced at my watch and swore when I saw it was already past my lunch hour. "I have to go, but you know, text me about where you want to meet for dinner," I said, then stopped when I realized I hadn't given him my number.

"Here, open your phone," I said, and Damian, still smiling, did as asked. I sent my information to him and then, without thinking, leaned down and kissed him again. I blushed when I realized I'd initiated a kiss this time and ran off before I did or said anything else embarrassing.

I ran back to the office, hoping my bosses wouldn't notice I was late. If I were lucky, Cary was taking his lunch break too; otherwise, there would be an interrogation there as well. I crossed the street and accidentally ran into a man at least the same height and build as Damian.

The man went to grab my arms as if to stop me from falling, but he gripped me so tight it hurt. "What... Stop!" I said and pulled back, almost falling into the traffic behind me. "What the hell?" I asked, about to lay into the man who'd all but attacked me.

No one was there. I rubbed my arms where he'd gripped me and looked around to see if anyone had noticed. No one was looking my way, so I rushed toward the office. If my arms didn't hurt, I'd say it'd been all my imagination.

The other part of my body that still tingled was my lips, where I'd kissed Damian only a few minutes before. I decided to ignore the weird attack and focus on the feel of those lips instead. I honestly couldn't wait until I got another chance to kiss him.

CHAPTER NINE

DAMIAN

I WATCHED OWEN SCURRY out of the deli and couldn't help the happy chuckle that escaped. The guy was so cute. I thought of what Molly had said the night before. Was he my type? I didn't know, really. I liked men who were shorter than me, thank goodness, because I hit six-four when I was still in high school. I was hardly ever not the tallest person around.

Besides, I don't think I'd ever gone out with someone like Owen. I pushed the thought aside. I wasn't one to focus on types. If I liked someone, I just went with it. I was very much like my dad in that way. When I'd come out to him all those years ago, he just shrugged. "If you like something, you like something. Makes no difference what I think."

I was hurt at the time, thinking he was belittling my sexuality. Of course, now I realize he was telling me he loved me no matter what and that it was my business who I liked.

I glanced down at the manilla envelope in front of me. I hadn't opened it in the office, mainly because the grumpy-looking lawyer had told me I wasn't supposed to. I hadn't thought to open it in front of Owen, but now, I wish I had.

I tore the seal and pulled out a strange parchment-type piece of paper. *'Touch the quill to the top of the page'* were the only words on the paper.

I looked inside the envelope and found a feather with a writing nib on the end like the one witches or wizards used in fantasy movies. I searched for ink, but finding none, I shrugged. "Might as well try it out," I said, not believing I'd be able to write with it.

The second I touched the quill to the paper, though, it began writing on its own. I jumped back, startled, and tried to stop it before I made a spectacle of myself. Several people glanced my way and gave me a strange look. Then I realized they were reacting at me and not at the quill.

When I calmed down, no one was actually staring at the strange feather quill writing away on the parchment. "So fucking weird," I whispered so no one could hear.

I tried to read the words, but with no luck. They didn't seem to be written in a language I recognized. I mean, it wasn't even an alphabet. It looked more like scratches and dashes. Almost like the ancient languages we studied in grade school. One of my teachers had been a massive fan of the Rick Riordan books, so he'd shown us ancient Greek writing, Egyptian hieroglyphics, and writing from the Middle East.

I watched with fascination as the quill wrote and wrote. Still, no one looked my way, so I sipped my soda and waited for the thing to stop.

Finally, after a very long time, it did, and the quill just fell over like it died or something. I reached with my right hand and picked up the paper to decipher the writing. Finally, I just gave up and slipped the quill back into the envelope. I picked the paper up in both hands to slip it into the envelope too, when my ring began to glow, and the words on the parchment began to transform.

Since ancient times, one individual, each generation, has been called to represent the legacy of the wizard. You have been called to fill this role. The quill and parchment are your lifeline, and you can use them to call upon the wizard who came before you. That wizard will help guide you through this lifetime.

My name was Elias Ericson, and I was born at the end of the First Great War. Upon my calling, I was forced to survive with nothing but the quill and parchment to guide me. No wizard may use their gifts to enhance their own prosperity. That's the first and most important law to understand.

If you try to use your gifts for personal gain, you will lose your power and put the entire universe at risk.

Fighting the dark forces who will inevitably come for you is difficult when your basic needs aren't met. Therefore, as your predecessor, I have striven to ensure you are better prepared to function in your new calling.

By now, you will have received the assets I have gifted to you. Before I begin to train you, understand that you will have plenty of money to function without having to work outside your calling. If my instincts are correct, that will be important as the dark will fall upon you harder than ever during my time.

There is transportation in the garage for you to use as well as the home. You should not need material things during your lifetime of service.

Besides struggling with financial concerns, I suffered great loneliness during my service as the Legacy Wizard. I do not wish that upon you. I have also planted the seeds of companionship for you. However, no one, not even a wizard as powerful as we, has the power to force someone to love another.

You will have to earn that love on your own, but hopefully, if my manipulations have been well placed, you will stumble upon a suitable mate to help you walk the often dangerous and treacherous journey ahead.

Legacy wizardry is primarily instinctual. You will learn to listen to and follow those instincts with your entire focus if you hope to survive. I will train you as much as possible, but ultimately, your inner thoughts will help you the most.

I will leave you with one final thought, the home I have given you is indeed special. I purchased it because it was already filled with the souls of those who had passed and wished to remain in service. You have nothing to fear from these individuals. Although, you should be warned their bark is often worse than their bite.

If they accept you, they will serve you as loyally as they have me.

Your style will inevitably differ from mine, and the home is enchanted to meet your needs. Of course, I couldn't do it myself, but since I have enchanted the house for you, my successor, I've taken the luxury of ensuring that your needs will be met.

For now, you should spend as much time in your new home as possible. Getting to know your servants and understanding that having clear boundaries will help ensure you have the space you need to hone your craft.

The room on top, in the attic, is further enchanted. You can use the space to train, learn, and recuperate. Only one spirit has access there, and his name is Orville. Please understand Orville is not the easiest spirit in your home to get along with, but he is the one you can trust with your life.

As your duties become more dire, you will need his help. So, please be patient with him.

Give yourself one full week in the home, get to know your servants, and allow Orville to introduce you to those willing to be known, and he will guide you. Place the quill back onto the parchment when you are ready to begin your instruction.

I've informed Orville to remind you of this instruction. I dare say that means he will be a bit more insistent than you may wish, but for your sake, you will need to train sooner rather than later, so forgive me for placing him in your way. Ultimately, you will appreciate the chance to begin your training early.

One can never know when the dark powers will attack. For some reason, each wizard is given a grace period. None before us have understood why. However, the grace period always ends sooner than we wish, and the first challenge of your powers is often the greatest.

Controlling the outcome decisively is the best course of keeping peace during your service.

I apologize, young wizard. I'm already going into teacher mode. Take your first week, enjoy your new home and your servants. The house is a fussy place with odd nuances, but it has served me well through my service. I can only hope it serves you as thoroughly.

Elias Ericson

I stared at the parchment long after I finished reading and then read it all again. Finally, the writing disappeared from the parchment, and I stored it back in the envelope with the quill.

The strange man in The Magic Shop had called me a wizard, but I hadn't understood what he'd meant. I didn't understand it now. I was supposed to be the wizard who replaced this

Elias guy who'd recently died. And spirits as servants? I mean, having seen the picture, I had to assume that was real.

Even having a name, I wasn't sure I felt any better about facing him. The idea of ghosts living in my home with me, especially when I knew they were there and could see them? Damn, I'm not sure I can handle that.

Trust your instincts had been the instruction. Right now, my instincts told me to go back to the house and meet these... What were they? Ghosts? Meet my servants. And I probably needed to do that before I brought my friends over.

I picked the envelope up and walked toward the exit. I paused when a strange-looking man stood across the street, watching the front of the deli. I could feel him staring at me, seeing me even though I was still inside the building.

Finally, he turned away and walked toward the end of the street. I'm not sure why, but it felt like he was saying "until later" in a threatening way. Trust your instincts? Right now, my instincts told me that man was no good.

They also told me I wasn't in danger, at least not yet. I left the deli, climbed into my car, and headed toward the Queen Anne neighborhood and the mansion I'd toured yesterday with Owen.

I scanned the area where the weird man had walked, but there was no evidence of him now. *At least that was good, right?*

The regal house sat in the Victorian neighborhood, almost inviting as I drove up to it today. Unlike yesterday when it was misty, the sunshine made all the difference as it shone off the multicolored paint.

I thought of my dad's apartment and then of the mansion. Would I be able to leave all I'd ever had and move into a level of opulence I'd never considered or even wanted? Would I be a fool not to want it?

The memory of the man staring at me moments before convinced me I might need any protection I could find. If the house gave me that, I'd be a fool not to take it. That propelled me out of the car and through the front gate.

I'd forgotten to lock the front door when we left yesterday, but it was locked tight when I tried to open it. I would've wondered who'd been here, but now, thanks to the magical parchment and quill, I assumed the ghost servants had closed and locked it.

Jeez, when had I begun to think of ghosts as normal? That was weird.

The house was spooky. I mean, knowing there were ghosts made it worse, but even not knowing, the place felt like it had been designed to be haunted. Would the spirits accept me? That was the real question.

I turned the key and walked in, expecting to see ghosts rushing around, dusting and stuff. Luckily, that didn't happen, but I still felt like someone was watching me. "Um," I said, leaving the door open so I could bolt if needed. "I guess I'm supposed to get to know you. Elias gave me this place. He said Orville could help me get to know you."

I heard movement above me, and a few moments later, I heard someone descending the stairs. I don't know how, but I could tell someone was standing in front of me. "Mr. Orville?" I asked.

Slowly, a figure began to take shape, like one of those strange lights popular during Halloween that made your window shades look like people were walking behind them.

"What is your name, sir?" the figure asked once he became solid enough to see.

"I'm...uh...I'm Damian Richards, and yours?" I asked.

"Orville is the name I go by now. You are the new Legacy Wizard, then?" he asked, walking around me as if assessing whether or not I was up to the task.

His behavior got my back up, and even though he was a freaking ghost, I still would've walked away or flipped the guy off had the parchment not told me this was typical.

"I suppose we will have to work with what we've got," he said and turned. "Come with me, and we'll try to make something of you."

I didn't move. I wouldn't allow someone to talk down to me—not even a ghost. Remembering the parchment said I needed boundaries, I stood rooted in place and waited for the ghost to turn around. "Listen," I said when he made eye contact, ignoring the shaking in my knees. "I realize you have been around a long time, and the parchment, Elias, said you can be trusted, but you will not be disrespectful to me, not if you wish me to work with you. Is that clear?" The ghost narrowed his eyes but nodded. "Good. Where would you like me to go?"

"I would like to introduce you to the rest of the staff, sir," he said, and I detected an air of respect that had been missing a moment earlier. Was that wishful thinking? Maybe, but at least I was standing up for myself.

Besides, if I were going to live here, and I wasn't sure I was going to, I wouldn't be talked down to—not by him or anyone else.

Chapter Ten

OWEN

I spent the afternoon finishing my paperwork, and by some miracle, another pile hadn't been added. I wasn't sure why but had to assume that was because I was working with Damian. Regardless of why, I was happy I'd have the weekend off, so I didn't dare mention it to anyone.

I texted Damian to find out when and where we should meet but hadn't heard back. Was he ghosting me already? I thought of the ghostly picture from his phone and smiled. I guess that gave new meaning to the word.

When the partners left a little before four, that was my cue to go as well. I waited a few minutes to make sure they didn't come back with a list of things for me to complete this weekend, and then I jumped up, grabbed my jacket, and dashed toward the front door.

"I'm off, Cary," I said as I walked through the door. I didn't turn around to see him, knowing he could easily be the one to add a bunch of crap to my to-do list. When the door closed behind me, I almost jumped up and down with relief.

I didn't use my app to order a car, but the walk from the office to Damian's place wasn't far. I could walk in that direction and enjoy all the historic homes along the way, and if he was there, great. If not, well, that was fine too. I could use the exercise.

The Queen Anne neighborhood was one of my favorites in Seattle. There's no way I could even afford a tiny one-bedroom apartment in the neighborhood, but I dreamed of one day owning something here or in Capitol Hill. Maybe one of the cute little bungalows with a garden in the front.

I imagined myself as a successful attorney, making enough to live in the neighborhood, when I came upon the old mansion house. The gate was open, which was strange, but I saw Damian's car sitting in the driveway and assumed he was home.

"You're his attorney, or at least, you work for his attorney," I said to myself, then took a deep breath and walked through the gate. I planned to tell him if he wasn't interested in me in any other way, we were fine. It's not like I expected someone like Damian to be interested in someone like me.

I reached the front door and knocked. It opened slowly. The only thing to make it scarier would be a creak, which this door didn't do. "Hello?" I called out.

No one responded, so I stepped closer. "Hello!" I called out again. I was just about to go in when the door slammed shut in my face, hitting me.

"Fuck!" I yelled as I fell back, gripping my nose.

"What the hell?" I heard Damian's voice as he pulled the door open. "Did they do that to you?"

"Dey?" I asked, the swelling already messing up my speech.

"Come here," he demanded and pulled me into the house. I quickly looked around to make sure there wasn't some kind of *they* around. But the room was empty. It must've been a draft that slammed the door shut. I knew old houses where I grew up did that sort of thing all the time.

Opening a different door or a window could cause a draft that would open a door, and closing it would make it slam shut. I let Damian pull me into the little powder room underneath the stairs. He used a washcloth to help me dab away the blood.

"I'm going to go to the kitchen to see if I can find some ice." I nodded as I tried to stop the bleeding. I looked in the mirror, and even through the tears from the swelling of my sinuses, from the size of it, I guessed my nose was probably broken.

Damian returned a few moments later with ice in a towel. "Here, hold this to your nose. You need to stop the swelling. Do you think it's broken?"

I nodded but didn't respond. My head was beginning to hurt now. "Come in here and sit down," he said, leading me out of the powder room and into the formal sitting room at the front of the house. I sat on a wooden chair, afraid I'd get blood on one of the pretty upholstered ones.

"Now, let me look closer," he said, and I let him pull the towel back. "Damn, yeah, I think it's broken too. Want me to drive you to the hospital?" he asked.

I nodded and was about to get up when Damian paused. "Really? How?" he asked, and I looked around the room.

"Huh?"

Damian blushed. "Um, I'll tell you in a moment." He looked to his left as if listening to someone, then turned back to me and sighed. "Listen, this is going to be bizarre for both of us, but I want to try something."

"Is it going to hurt?" I asked, thinking maybe he would try to set my nose himself.

"I-I don't know," he said, looking to his left again. "The consensus is that it won't. It's probably nonsense, but let's try."

Damian closed his eyes and lifted his hands. They cupped my nose, he began to hum, and then his eyes flew open. They were both solid white, and I just about jumped out of my seat, but something held me in place.

I wanted to scream, run, but I couldn't do a damned thing.

Seconds passed, and Damian's eyes returned to normal. Then he lowered his hands. "Wow," he said when he examined my nose.

Whatever held me down loosened, so I jumped up, dropping the bloody towel to the floor. I rushed toward the door, but Damian stopped me. "Wait, don't freak out. I can explain."

"Explain what? Are you possessed or something? I need to get out of here. You too. You should leave this house."

Just then, three apparitions appeared in front of me. I recognized the one in the middle first. It was the man from Damian's photo. "What the hell?" I asked as I came to a stop in front of them.

"I'm sorry, sir. I'm Orville, this is Alice, and this is Emma," he said, but I was too stunned to move, much less respond.

"I-I'm sorry, sir," the apparition named Alice said. "I didn't mean to hit you in the face."

I looked at Damian, who shrugged. "I just met them all today myself," Damian said.

"Ghosts? You're talking to the house's ghosts?"

"And why wouldn't he?" Orville asked indignantly.

"First of all, there's not supposed to be ghosts, and second, you attacked me. And...and your eyes, something must've possessed you. This isn't okay. You need to let me leave."

"No one possessed him. He's a wizard, and he was using his powers and a mighty fine job he did of it. Look here, in the mirror," Orville said, pointing toward an oval wooden framed mirror on the wall above a sideboard.

I gulped, afraid to look away from the apparitions in case one of them attacked me again, but I couldn't resist looking where he pointed either. I saw myself in the mirror, and there was blood under my nose, but the swelling was gone. It looked as if nothing had happened but a simple nosebleed.

Ignoring the ghosts, more intrigued by what I saw in the mirror than the fear of them, I went to get a closer look, reaching up and feeling my nose. It was fixed. Not even tender.

"H-how?" I asked, turning toward Damian, who just shrugged.

"No idea, it just happened, but it worked, right? Your nose isn't broken now?"

I looked at him for a few seconds and then back at the mirror, then turned to where the ghosts stood. "Why did you attack me?" I asked the female spirit, Alice, as the male ghost had called her.

"I didn't mean to. I saw the door was open, and you were coming in, and I tried to close it before you could trespass."

"Trespass? I was here yesterday."

"I know, sir. I just didn't recognize you."

"Alice, please go to your quarters. Let me spend some time with our guest. You too, Emma," Orville said.

Both female ghosts disappeared, and I felt a slight breeze indicating they'd just walked past. Of course, the hairs on the back of my neck stood on end. "What's going on? I don't understand any of this."

Damian stepped forward and put his hand on my elbow. "I think I can explain some of it. After you left the sandwich place, I found a piece of parchment and a quill in the envelope your boss gave me this morning. It gave me instructions about the home, about Orville," he said, gesturing toward the ghost who stood before me.

"Orville is a servant to the home. My predecessor, who left the place to me in his will, said I should spend time with Orville and the other ghosts. They're here to help me fulfill some destiny I have."

"Destiny?" I asked stupidly, not knowing how to respond to it all.

"Yeah, I guess I'm supposed to be some legacy wizard. I don't know. I'm still figuring it all out."

"Why did your eyes turn white? That was freaky," I asked, and Damian shrugged.

Orville stepped forward. "When the power comes through the wizard, or at least this is how it was with his predecessor and clearly how it happened just a moment ago, it can be drawn from parts of the wizard's being. More often than not, in a healing, the wizard lends his own essence to the person he is healing. In this case, your nose was broken, so the power flowed from Mr. Richard's face—his eyes in particular, as the nose and eyes are closely related, are they not?"

I nodded and realized I was talking to a ghost. I was getting an explanation of what happened from a fucking ghost. I was losing my mind, except, apparently, so was Damian.

"I don't get any of this, the ghosts. Do you have...what? Magic powers or something?"

Damian laughed. "Do I get a wand?" he asked Orville, whose eyes shot open. "I should say not. You aren't a witch. You're a wizard. Wand indeed."

"I like wands," Damian said, and I snorted at how preposterous the whole thing was.

"Okay, I need a drink. Damian, I'll see you later."

"Wait," Damian said. "Don't go. I-I wanted to spend time with you, and now you're the only person I know who's experienced all this," he said, waving his hands around the room, "except me. It helps me feel less crazy."

"Your predecessor left a very fine scotch in the library if you'd like to share that with your guest," Orville said, gesturing toward the room to his right.

"Do you like scotch?" Damian asked.

I laughed. "Not that much, but right now, it sounds good enough."

"Good enough," Orville spat out then seemed to catch himself. "We have other spirits as well," he said, leaving us in the entryway. I looked at Damian, and both of us snickered.

"They do indeed," Damian said.

CHAPTER ELEVEN

DAMIAN

WHEN WE'D TOURED THE home yesterday, there had been no liquor in the cabinets. Now, however, when Orville opened them, they were full. "Wow," Owen said. "We looked in there yesterday, didn't we?"

Orville smiled. "We weren't sure who you were yesterday, so we hid the contents of the house, just in case Mr. Ericson's solicitor would see fit to meddle."

Owen laughed. "I am officially one of Damian's solicitors, so you guessed correctly." He studied the contents of the cabinet and smiled. "I'll have a whiskey. To be honest, meeting ghosts seems to require the hard stuff."

"As you wish," Orville said formally, pouring Owen a drink. "You, sir?" he asked me, and I shrugged.

"I think the same is fine."

Orville poured my drink and replaced the bottle. "If you need me, sir, just call my name. I need to console Alice," he said, glancing at Owen as if he were frustrated that Owen's nose had been broken by the ghost woman slamming the door in his face.

It was all so strange. When Orville disappeared, I reached out and placed my hand over Owen's. "Are you okay?"

Owen shook his head while pursing his lips. "Oh no, not even remotely okay. I had my nose broken by a ghost. Then you healed my nose with some weird juju magic. Then another ghost served me some pretty amazing whiskey, a brand my uncle drinks, but only on special occasions. I know for a fact it costs a fortune. In fact, Damian, I recognize most of those bottles, and they all cost a fortune," he said, pointing toward the closed cabinet. "You have bougie ghosts serving bougie drinks in your bougie house. For real, do you think I'm going to be okay?"

I laughed. "Does it help that I'm just as weirded out as you? Apparently, I'm some storybook wizard thingy."

Owen turned his hand over and took mine. "Okay, so this is very strange. At least you now know who fixed the vase yesterday. How many more ghosts are here?"

I choked. "I don't think I want to know, but luckily, I won't have to do anything to keep the place up. They have gardeners, people who keep up with maintenance, um, dead people, but they all have jobs. It's weird."

"They don't scare you?" he asked.

I shrugged. "At first, yeah, but to be honest, I've met a lot of them today, and they don't seem scary. I can also tell when they're in the room, so, like now, it's just us. If I couldn't, I'd be more paranoid."

"Yeah, can you do your wizard thing so I can do that too?"

"Sure," I said without thinking and waved my hand. Owen's eyes glowed this time instead of mine. I don't think he noticed, and I honestly didn't mean to do it. It just came out. I knew how to, and without thinking, I did.

Just then, Alice came back into the room. I could tell she didn't mean to be seen, but both Owen and I turned toward her. "Oh, um, sorry, I...Orville said I should speak to Mr. Owen again. To ensure he is okay."

"I'm fine, Alice. I know it was an accident now, but thanks for checking."

The ghost's eyes grew large, but she bowed, quickly walking through the wall and disappearing.

"I don't think she knew you could see or hear her. Apparently, the whole waving my hand thing worked."

I heard my phone ring and pulled it out of my pocket. "Shit, that's Molly. They're headed over."

"Wow, have you warned your, um, ghost people? You don't want to have to fix more broken noses."

I quickly nodded at Owen. "True," I said. "Orville," I called out, and the ghost immediately appeared.

"I have friends coming over to see the house. Can you make sure no one else gets hurt?"

Orville nodded. "Shall I remove the personal items again, sir?" he asked, and I laughed.

"Oh, yeah, you should," I said and was glad of Orville's perceptive abilities. My...okay, they weren't really my friends. Molly's friends were borderline kleptomaniacs when it came to anything they perceived as otherworldly.

Orville bowed and disappeared, and I could hear things like the drinks in the cabinet being moved. I couldn't see them, which meant they operated behind the walls. I shivered slightly, wondering just how many spirits occupied the house. That was something I would want to figure out sooner rather than later.

I don't think I minded living with ghosts, but I wanted to know how many were there, and at some point, I wanted to meet them all. If they were going to be my roommates, I sure as hell wanted a handle on whether any of them were dangerous.

Chapter Twelve

OWEN

Damian's friends were strange. I mean, it was weird to meet a bunch of dead people who lived in his new house, but honestly, that was less weird than dealing with this group.

I liked Molly though. She was gregarious and full of life. Clearly, she was the leader of the little tribe that'd shown up tonight.

I watched as the house's spirits came and went through the night. None of them paid much attention to the group of black-clad figures who took turns telling us they felt certain spirits in the room. One arrogant guy kept saying he was feeling a bunch of minors in the room. The only person in there was Emma, who giggled at his proclamation before disappearing.

One of the people, Shadow, who had given me her card the night before, seemed to sense the ghosts. When a ghost I hadn't met, some young man dressed in clothes from the early 1900s, walked by as we explored the second floor, Shadow paused and looked right at where the guy had been.

I logged that in my mind because it seemed important for future reference. Although, I had no idea why. I doubted I'd ever know any of these people very well. For one, I had very little in common with them, and second, I didn't like most of them.

It was one thing to be like Shadow, feel the presence of ghosts, and not respond. It was another to pretend you had all the answers. Unfortunately, most of the group fell into that second category.

I noticed Damian didn't offer to show anyone the attic. I thought he was right about that. I wasn't a wizard or witch nor had any claim to powers except whatever Damian had done. Even I could tell the attic was a protected space. Not something for outsiders.

When Molly announced we should have a séance in the dining room, I glanced over to find Orville standing at attention. I cocked my eyebrow, hoping that sent a nonverbal question as to whether that would cause problems. He seemed to understand and rolled his eyes, telling me it would be a harmless exercise.

In fact, he couldn't have been farther from the truth. Molly turned the lights off and lit a candle I'd watched Orville add to a drawer just for the occasion. Then Molly told us to join hands. They all began humming the same note, and Molly told us to close our eyes.

"Spirits of this home come to us, come and be with us this night."

At first, nothing happened, but then I saw Emma floating through the wall. She was gripping her throat in a way that made me think she was in pain. When she got to the middle of the table, she laughed out loud and quickly disappeared through the side wall.

One by one, the ghosts I hadn't met mimicked her. I glanced at Damian just as a trio of ghosts came in and began doing a bizarre dance above the candle after one of the participants began singing some off-tune, made-up song about spirits feeling welcome.

It was so over the top that Damian and I snickered, which earned a hateful look from most of the people in the group.

Molly ended the seance shortly after and shooed everyone out of the house. One of the Goth guys was the last, and he turned to look at us before he left. "You shouldn't scoff at things you don't understand. The spirit world is real, and they take your attitudes very seriously."

I bit my tongue literally as images of the ghost's shenanigans filled my memory. "Oh boy, if he only knew," I said after he stormed out of the room.

Molly walked around us, studying both of us for several moments. "You're up to something or know something you aren't sharing. Don't worry. I may not be magical or have the gifts others do, but I can pry the truth out of anyone. I'll figure out what you two are up to," she said, but her smile showed she was mostly teasing.

She hugged Damian and cocked an eyebrow at me when I didn't follow her, but she shook my hand before heading out.

"That was fun," Damian said.

I laughed. "I like your ghosts a lot more than I did earlier," I said as I reached up and rubbed my nose.

"Yeah, me too."

"I should probably get going," I said, but before I could leave, Damian reached over and took me in his arms. "Can I kiss you at least once before you go?" he asked.

I nodded, dumbfounded, as his gorgeous face closed the distance between us. When his lips touched mine, I felt like my brain exploded. I wanted this man so much. He was like some bizarre drug.

When we pulled apart, I had to look down to catch my breath. "Want to spend the night?" he asked.

"Like here, with all these, um, people?" I asked.

"Or we could go back to my apartment."

Yes, my brain screamed, but I sighed and shook my head. "Listen, Damian, I like you, a lot actually, and in my experience one-night stands never go further than that. Wouldn't you rather, you know, take things slower, get to know each other before we cross that bridge?"

Damian scooted his large frame closer to mine but smiled before kissing me again. "I think getting to know you would be fun, but I don't have any rules about what parts of you I get to know first."

I laughed and almost said yes. Then I caught sight of one of the ghosts as they slipped through the wall behind us. *Emma.* I was almost sure it was Emma.

I shook my head and kissed him. "We have an audience here, and that's not something I'm into. Rain check?" I asked.

Damian frowned. "I wish I hadn't done whatever I did to show you the ghosts."

I laughed again. "Good night, Damian," I said, and he moved back so I could open the door.

"Good night, handsome," Damian said, gently closing the door behind me.

CHAPTER THIRTEEN

DAMIAN

WHEN ORVILLE APPEARED BEHIND me, it seemed as if he was ready to be chastised. I laughed instead. "That was funny. Thank all the ghosts here for that display. I haven't had that much fun with those blowhards in, well, ever."

Orville looked perplexed for a moment, then smiled. "We aren't used to people seeing us. I noticed you gave that power to your companion as well."

"Companion? Who Owen? No, he's someone I just met, but I like him. Why? Are you going to do some weird homophobic ghost attitude on me now? 'Cause, dude, that shit won't fly."

Orville cringed. "No need for profanity, sir. No, you'll find that anyone here will have given up such notions of propriety shortly after death. Love and companionship are often difficult to find and even more difficult to hold onto. You will find no judgment amongst the residents of this home, sir."

I nodded. "Good." I paused, then sighed. "Orville, I'm going to need privacy if I'm going to live here. It sounds like some of you either live in the walls or at least go through them, which means I can't see you. That's too strange for me."

"I assure you, sir, we all understand that the living need such things," Orville said, then paused before continuing. "I don't think any of the residents here would intentionally bother you, sir, but we aren't used to worrying about appearances these days. Mr. Ericson was able to create barriers when he needed privacy, and I have always been the only one allowed in the attic space. I understand you have access to the quill and parchment, which I should've already told you should be stored in the attic, as it's your lifeline between your predecessor and yourself. The attic is the one place you have that exists outside of this space and time. When you need sanctuary, you will find it there. Maybe you should ask Mr. Ericson how to create the boundaries to ensure you maintain your privacy."

I nodded, then walked up the stairs toward the attic. "Thank you, Orville," I said. "We got off to a bumpy start today, but now I've spent the day with you, I'm glad you're here. I think I'll also enjoy the other residents once I get to *know* everyone."

I emphasized the know, hoping he understood my meaning. When he bowed and turned away, I walked up the stairs, letting the door close.

The attic felt much more welcoming. Okay, welcoming wasn't the word. It still felt foreign. This house didn't feel like home. It felt like a stranger's house, but it also felt like it was mine as well. I had brought the manila envelope with me into the house and left it on the table on the landing right outside the attic's stairway.

I'd grabbed it on the way up the stairs, and now I was in the attic, I went to the ancient-looking library table under the Lake Washington window, which was so dark now I couldn't see its design.

I pulled the parchment out and placed the quill in a holder I instinctively knew it belonged with. I yawned deeply and realized I wasn't in the mood for more discussion with ghosts, be they the ones who occupied the house or the one who talked through the parchment and quill. I was just about to go back downstairs to leave when I noticed a little bed in one of the alcoves.

How would it be to sleep here tonight? I didn't have to think twice. I knew just like I'd known how to heal Owen that the bed was clean. I also knew I was alone and that Orville wouldn't bother me up here, so I stripped off my clothes and climbed into the bed.

"Memory foam?" I asked as I crawled under the covers. I hadn't expected the mattress to be modern or to have a new smell. I smiled, realizing this was part of what the parchment had told me. My predecessor had gone to great lengths to ensure I'd be comfortable.

I fell asleep the moment my head hit the pillow. I dreamed so much that night about the house, the design, and the décor changing as I walked through it. I kept seeing the ancient, uncomfortable-looking furniture turning modern.

The kitchen went from sterile and boring to something viewers saw on television after someone had it renovated. I wasn't one to worry about design. Frankly, I never thought I'd own anything that required something like that.

However, as I dreamed of all the changes, I knew if I stayed here, and I was beginning to like that idea more and more, I would definitely be making it more my own style.

Chapter Fourteen

OWEN

I whistled as I entered my apartment after the taxi dropped me off. From the moment Damian walked into my office, it'd been a strange couple of days, but it was a nice sort of strange.

No, it was a freaking awesome sort of strange. Wizards and ghosts existed. I didn't think I'd ever spent much time thinking about that. When I was young, I imagined going to Hogwarts, just like any other kid back then, but I clearly didn't get into it as much as Damian's friends. They were so over the top about it and so wrong as well.

The silly behavior of the ghosts had been humorous. I could only imagine how hard it would be to have the living around, especially if they were pretending nonsense like the group tonight were.

Then again, I doubted those ghosts had experienced much human silliness since an actual wizard had lived in the home before Damian.

I got why they made fun of it all, and to be honest, it helped me stop being so afraid of them, although when the ghost disappeared through the wall when I'd been kissing Damian, it sent a cold chill through me.

I crawled into my bed and pulled the covers up to my chin, knowing it would get chilly before morning. I never minded that kind of cold at night though. To be honest, I preferred it. I hated being cold during the day, but at night, there wasn't much more wonderful than cuddling under a big pile of blankets.

In fact, I couldn't help but imagine cuddling with a certain wizard under the pile of blankets. Damian was clearly interested. That was obvious in the way he kissed me tonight.

I woke up feeling so happy the following day. I don't remember dreaming, but I had to assume it was good stuff, considering how good I felt.

I got out of bed, once again happy I did not need to work this weekend. I almost skipped a shower, thinking it might be a good grunge day, but then I hoped Damian might text and want to go out. So, I jumped in the shower and dressed.

When I glanced at my phone, it felt like my whole body smiled when I saw the text from Damian.

> Him: You will not believe what happened here last night.

> Me: Ghosts. You met more ghosts? Or did you find new ways to use your powers?

> Him: Can you come over? You won't believe me if I just tell you.

I paused and then did a happy dance before I texted him back.

> Me: Sure. I'll grab a taxi.

> Him: No. Jeez, I forgot you don't have a car. I'll come get you. Hold tight.

I almost texted him that there was no need, but the thought of him coming to get me and taking care of me felt good.

> Me: You sure? I can just hire a taxi.

> Him: Yeah. I'm still a professional driver, so you can give me a tip later.

I laughed when the GIF of the cartoon character waggling his eyes came up.

I sent back a thumbs-up and went to brush my teeth. I almost dashed out of my apartment to get coffee, but I figured he'd let me treat him, so I waited until he arrived.

"Hey," I said, slipping into his front seat.

"Hey," he said, leaning over and inviting me to kiss him. Of course, I didn't hesitate to take him up on the invitation.

I moaned happily as he pulled back. "So, you're going to be amazed at what happened."

"Cool, what?" I asked.

"Trust me, it's a show and tell, not a tell and show thing. Do you need coffee?" he asked.

I smiled. "The force is strong with you," I said, mimicking the *Star Wars* reference and getting an eye roll from him. "Yes, please, I need coffee. I figured I could treat us both."

He pulled into traffic, and we stopped at a strange little shop I hadn't been to before. He parked in front of the building, and when we got to the front, he said, "The day I met you, I came here by accident. I'd never been before. But it wasn't a coffee shop. It was a different building, and it said Magic Shop on the front. That's how all this started. Then, when I came back out, it had transformed into this."

I looked at the facade and shrugged. "Not much to look at," I said.

"True, but the coffee is so good. Come on. I'll show you."

We walked in, and I ordered my regular almond milk latte, and he ordered a cappuccino. The place wasn't crowded like it should be at this time of day in winter. I grabbed a muffin to split with Damian, and when the coffee was done, we went to sit by the front window.

I halved the muffin and then took a drink. "Wow," I said, my eyes growing wide. "This is like the best coffee in Seattle. Why isn't this place packed?"

"I might be new to all this, but I'm going to guess this is how they want it."

I looked over at the barista, a petite woman who appeared to be our age. She winked at me like she'd heard what Damian just said. It had to be magic if she did because we were on the other side of the room.

I made a mental note to keep my thoughts to myself in a world where people had superhero hearing.

"So, what did you want to show me?" I asked as Damian took a big bite of his share of the muffin.

When he swallowed, he sighed. "You really should see it to believe it, but I'll tell you this much: last night, I slept in the attic, and this morning, when I woke up, the house had changed."

I cocked an eyebrow. "Like, how did it change?" I asked.

He tossed the rest of the muffin in his mouth, chewed, and swallowed. "Come on, I'll show you," he said, forcing me to wrap my half of the muffin since I had yet to take a bite and grab my coffee to follow him out.

He told me he didn't mind if I ate in the car, so I finished the muffin on the way to his house. The house looked exactly the same to me.

"What's different?" I asked.

He just laughed. "Not on the outside. Come with me," he said, leading the way up to the porch.

He didn't use his key, but I heard the door unlatch when he turned the knob, clearly unlocking on its own. So bizarre.

When I walked in, I froze. The traditional layout was similar. The smaller rooms were still to the sides, with pocket doors leading to them, but where the dining room had been with walls separating the kitchen and butler's pantry, it was now open to the entryway.

"H-how?" I asked.

"Magic," Orville said as he drifted through the wall to our right.

"Magic? Can ghosts do magic?" I asked, and for the first time since I'd met him, Orville chuckled.

"That's a no, but Mr. Richards certainly can. However, I don't suspect this was done by you, sir," he said, addressing Damian. "I'm guessing this was a spell cast by Mr. Ericson, your predecessor."

"I dreamed it all," Damian said. "All night, I dreamed and saw the changes in my mind, but I had no idea they were happening."

"Well," I said, walking toward the now open-concept kitchen and dining area. "I approve of your dream design. This is beautiful. Oh," I said as I noticed the butler's pantry shelving was still intact, although the walls around it weren't. "You saved the old shelving."

Damian nodded. "Yeah, I saw something like this on a TV renovation series and remembered how much I loved it. It must've registered in my dream because this is how it was left."

I walked around the kitchen, admiring the intricacy. I had to imagine only a dream could come up with some of the whimsical elements. You had to look close to see the legs of the island splayed out to show unicorns on the ends.

My spirits lifted with the sight of the unicorns, and I smiled, thinking how much I'd always loved them. My room back home had been filled to the ceiling with stuffed unicorns until I'd started dating the hateful Mr. Strange. "I love it," I said, forcing the nasty thoughts of my ex out of my head. "Was the kitchen the only thing you did?"

"No, come into this room," Damian said, leading us into the parlor, which was still separated from the dining room with the same door. The room was still traditional and a little formal, but the old furniture had been replaced with more comfortable and modern pieces. It still matched the home's style, although if I were designing it, I'd probably have stuck with the formal stuff and turned the other rooms into the informal ones.

We walked through each room, and it was easy to see which ones Damian didn't care much about. The music room now had a fancy sound system and was super modern, which was sad. I didn't like old homes that had lost their historical charm.

The library was the biggest transformation. The shelves still held all the books, but the natural wood had been painted. "Ugh," I said before I realized I was saying that out loud.

"You don't like it?" Damian asked.

I forced a smile on my face. "I do, but it was so grand before. I liked the wood, but this isn't my home, it's yours, and the design and craftsmanship is well done."

I noticed Orville watching me, his face impassive, but I also got the impression he agreed with my assessment. "What did you do with the upstairs?" I asked.

Damian shook his head. "I don't think I did anything. I haven't paid much attention to those rooms, and they weren't in my dreams."

I thought for a moment, then decided to take the bull by the horns. "Let me ask, will you ever have a lot of guests over?" I asked.

Damian shook his head. "Probably not. Why?"

"What about kids? Do you want a lot of children?"

Damian laughed. "No, not even if I were straight and could make them myself. I'm not one for raising kids."

I turned to Orville. "Do any of the ghosts, um, other residents, live in those rooms? Or are they mostly empty?"

Orville shrugged. "Most of the residents have established rooms in the basement. Others are distributed around other parts of the structure. No one uses the rooms on the second floor, not even the former wizard himself used them."

I smiled. "Come with me," I said as I led the way up the stairs to the second floor. "If you aren't going to use the second floor for guest rooms or your own family, why don't you create the modern living space up here? Especially if you've got the magic powers to do it." I said. We walked through the rooms, and I pointed out how he could turn them into a large living room, with a television and sound systems, that he could use without disturbing the historical integrity of the first floor."

The more I talked, the happier Damian got. "I can see it, and yes, I like that too. It felt strange moving things around. He waved his hands to create it, then froze. "Oops, I forgot, I'm not supposed to use my powers for personal gain."

"I guess you'll have to sleep on it," I said, and Damian chuckled.

"Literally," he said, and before I knew it, he embraced me and kissed me again.

"Hopefully, I can return the first floor to what it was and then turn this into my living space. Which reminds me, Orville, what's the room off the kitchen?" Damian asked.

"Aah, it's a multitude of things, but things you shouldn't worry about yet. Mr. Ericson didn't want you to worry about all that until you were settled. Why don't you and Mr. Lloyd go collect your things? Once you have moved them to the residence, we can help you unpack."

"Oh, okay," Damian said, but I could tell he wasn't quite ready.

"Why don't we go over to your old place and assess the situation? There's no hurry to move in yet, is there?" I asked, and Orville's face showed that, in fact, there might be.

I didn't acknowledge his expression though. Something more was cooking here, and it wasn't my place to intervene, but yeah, if I could help smooth the transition, I'd happily do it.

As we drove to Damian's apartment, I thought again how serendipitous it was that I didn't have to work this weekend. Then I realized it probably wasn't a coincidence.

I smiled when I saw Damian's apartment. It was exactly what I imagined. I could see the rough edges I'd seen in the man I'd only just met but had begun to feel attached to. We walked around, and I couldn't help but feel how hard it would be to change, to leave, especially when he showed me his dad's belongings.

When we sat down on the worn furniture in his living room, I took his hand. "Listen, Damian, I'm not magical, but I am perceptive. I've always had that skill. I feel you need to transition sooner rather than later, and when we discussed that before, I could tell Orville wanted to say the same. Could you magic this stuff over to your new home?" I asked.

Damian chuckled. "No. I don't think so. I'm not sure it would be considered my gain to do so. I... When... Well, you know, when I was going to try to change the second floor when you talked about it earlier, I felt an instant need to stop. I think there's a fail-safe that keeps me from, you know, screwing up and doing magic I'm not supposed to."

I smiled. "Why don't you try to move the apartment over to the second floor of your new home? You can change things around once it's there, and if you're not supposed to do that with magic, you have a house full of ghosts who seem keen to help."

CHAPTER FIFTEEN

DAMIAN

O WEN'S CALM DEMEANOR WAS exactly what I needed. Dad had barely kept the rent paid when I was growing up, and now, with this being in an up-and-coming neighborhood, the landlord had raised the rent three times in the last four years. I would rather not give the leach another penny, but I wasn't ready to get rid of dad's or my stuff either.

When Owen was talking about the second floor, I was picturing a fancy living space, but now, I was imagining this, my life, moved into that one. I liked it instantly.

"Can, um, can you hold my hands while I try? I might need moral support. There are a lot of memories between these walls."

Owen didn't hesitate but reached over and took my hands. I closed my eyes, and the world began to spin. I'm not sure what I expected, but I wasn't transferring furniture like we'd planned. Instead, I was spinning through space with Owen.

It was almost exactly like my dreams last night. Both real and a vision all at once. We instantly stood together in front of the house, looking from the front door to the back. It was different from this morning's transformation, although some of those elements still existed. The biggest difference was that Owen was now as much a part of the place as I was.

I could feel elements of him in the design. So much of it traditional, but with sweet little additions that made the home feel modern and happy. The parlor had a mix of this morning's furniture as well as some of the old. A fire burned happily in the original fireplace.

I turned toward the music room that now housed a self-playing, baby grand piano with comfortable, modern, but formal seating. The kitchen and dining room were exactly as they had been, but the library was back to its original wood shelving and formal green carpeting. I instantly knew this was right. It was precisely how it should've been from the beginning.

We seemed to glide up the stairs together, and the bedrooms had been totally transformed. It was now a living space, as Owen had suggested, but with a much more modern design. I saw my dad's old leather chair in the corner next to a fireplace, identical to the placement of the one downstairs, and a nostalgic fire burned warmly inside it.

I looked around the space and saw myself there. Things I'd loved my entire life were there, but everything looked new and modern, not torn or broken like most of my furniture had been in the apartment.

There were no bedrooms though. Not downstairs, not on this floor. I looked at the attic door, which opened, and Owen and I floated up the staircase into the attic.

It was so different yet very much the same. The space was still open like before, but on one side was a king-size bed that sat snugly under one of the great windows. The bathroom where I'd cleaned off the blood when I'd broken the ugly vase was transformed. Now, it was modern and chic. Nothing like the dusty room had been before.

A considerable closet was attached to the back, and my and Owen's clothes hung there.

The vision changed then, and when I opened my eyes, the apartment was empty. Owen and I were sitting on the floor instead of the worn leather furniture that'd been here before.

"Um," Owen said, his eyes wide. "I think I might have injected myself into your moving vision. I hope I didn't screw up."

I pulled him into my side. Seeing all my stuff so beautifully upgraded and stored in my new space and now seeing Dad's and my apartment empty made me emotional.

"Come on, let's see what happened at the house," I finally said.

Owen just nodded, but I could tell he was upset. I wasn't quite sure why. Sure, we'd shared a vision, and yeah, I could see how he'd put himself in the space, and even if his clothes ended up in my closet, that wasn't so bad. We could move them back. The powers prevented me from doing stuff for my own gain, not helping him fix stuff that happened in a vision.

Besides, I liked his style. The first floor of the home in the vision was so comfortable and inviting. I could see many nights sitting in front of the fire, reading a book or drinking a cocktail in the warm library. Hell, maybe we could even hire a real musician to play that fancy grand piano and not just rely on the self-playing element.

It'd all be good, no matter what.

Owen said he would give me some space, which, truth be known, I needed. I wandered through the tiny apartment, amazed at how small it felt now it was empty. "Dad," I said, knowing that, unlike the ghosts in the mansion, my dad was no longer here, "I guess I'm finally flying the nest."

A calmness fell over me, and although I couldn't see his spirit, I'd been wrong. My father was here, and he was giving me his blessing.

A tear slid down my cheek as I said one last goodbye, then closed and locked the door. Our lease was mostly nonexistent. We'd lived here too long, and Dad had refused to sign another one even though he'd paid the upped rent to keep us from getting kicked out.

I texted the greedy jerk of a landlord, letting him know I'd moved out. "The apartment is yours," I wrote, then shoved the key under the door. I have no idea where Dad's key went. It was probably with the stuff that was transferred to the new home.

As soon as I had that thought, I saw the key sitting in a cabinet and knew exactly where it was.

I could've had it come to me and left it for the landlord, but I decided against it. Instead, I could see the key mounted in a small picture frame and placed on the wall in the attic next to where all the old books were stored.

No matter how amazing my new home was, that key would always represent home to me, even more than the empty apartment I'd just left. I knew I'd cherish that for the rest of my life.

Chapter Sixteen

OWEN

I WAS SO EMBARRASSED. This was Damian's vision, his life, and his future, and somehow, I'd imposed myself onto it. When I looked around and saw the empty apartment, I knew the vision I'd seen of his new home, with all my stupid design elements tucked here and there, would be reality.

Worse, so much worse, were my clothes and belongings. I'd known Damian for all of three days—not even that long—and I'd thrust myself into his life, into his home. I was mortified.

I left him alone, mostly because I knew he needed the time, and found a little coffee food truck not more than a block from his apartment. I got us the same coffees we'd ordered this morning. When I returned, he was already waiting for me. "You got me coffee?" he asked, smiling.

I nodded and handed it to him. "Come on, then. Let's see if my stuff made it to the house. Hey, what did you see while we were holding hands?" he asked.

I sighed as I climbed into the passenger side of his car. "I'm so sorry, Damian. I-I saw my stuff in your home. I don't know if it's at your house. Maybe, hopefully, it's not, but I kinda get the feeling it is. We'll have to move it all back to my apartment if it is. I mean, it's not like I own a lot of stuff, you know. I've only been in Seattle for a few months, and I didn't bring much with me, and—"

"Owen," Damian said, interrupting me. "It's okay. You didn't do anything wrong. Let's go see what happened."

I nodded and took a drink of my coffee, willing it to calm my nerves. Yeah, I liked Damian. I liked him a lot, but I wasn't someone to jump into a relationship. Damian hadn't asked if I wanted to live with him. I hadn't agreed to live with him. I just wanted to help him transfer his belongings.

The magic thing was new to me, although I was beginning to wonder why it wasn't freaking me out more. In college, I'd taken a world's religions class, and we'd studied about reincarnation, which resonated with me. I mean, recycled spirits made sense, especially now that I'd met actual dead people.

I wondered if maybe my soul had experienced magic before for me to be so calm about it now.

I sighed as Damian pulled into his driveway, the old iron gate closing behind him. This home truly was amazing. I also knew this home was worth megabucks.

I followed Damian into the house. He was all but skipping to get inside and see it. I was anything but excited. Reticent, if I was being honest.

Sure enough, the moment we walked in, the pocket doors were all standing open, allowing us to see all the rooms at once. I groaned when I saw the Irving Shapiro watercolor my grandfather had left me in his will, now hanging over the fireplace. The painting hadn't even come to Seattle with me. My mom was going to come unglued when she found it missing.

I groaned when the little bronze statue of a unicorn, something I knew I'd given to charity, sat on the mantle in the library. Ugh, again and again, as I saw my personal belongings interspersed throughout the rooms. "Oh, I'm so sorry, Damian," I said again when I turned and saw his smiling face.

"Come upstairs. I want to see my stuff up there," he said, and I reluctantly followed him.

Whereas my stuff shouldn't be in the house, the transformation to this floor was amazing. It was like some home design star had come in and planned the space, reupholstered his old furniture, and placed it in the rooms to maximize their beauty, making the space a comfortable mix of rustic and modern.

I didn't say anything, but I was so happy the first floor was traditional again, although I sure as hell intended to get help moving all my own stuff back to my freaking place soon.

"It's beautiful, Damian. It feels so, well, like you? Can I say that after only knowing you a few days?"

Damian came over and embraced me. "You can say it over and over 'cause it's correct. This is better than I ever could've hoped for, and I think I owe you for it all."

I sighed but felt happy for him. "Come on, let's go to the attic."

I let him pull me up the stairs. I stared at the space. It was exactly how I'd seen it in my mind. I didn't linger, only went toward the bedroom and new bath before slipping into the gigantic closet. "Ugh," I groaned again. "Damian, my clothes are here," I said. "I'm so sorry."

Damian laughed and again embraced me from behind, "Don't worry, I'm sure we can work it out," he said as my phone rang.

I saw it was my landlady and cringed. "I better take this. She's going to be wondering why all my belongings disappeared, although I have no idea what I'm going to say to her."

"Hello?" I answered.

"Oh, hi Owen, good news. A couple just viewed your apartment and want to take it tomorrow. I already had them sign the lease. I was surprised you wanted to move after such a short time, but I guess this was just serendipitous. Congratulations! I'll return your deposit and the prorated rent. Oh, and thanks for doing such a good job cleaning it out. I swear it's better now than when you moved in."

She hung up without waiting for a response, and I stared at Damian, my mouth hanging open.

"What's wrong?" Damian asked.

"Um, I guess you just got a roommate."

CHAPTER SEVENTEEN

DAMIAN

T HE WORDS OF THE parchment came back to me. "I have planted the seeds of companionship for you." It looked as if Owen was about to cry, but I just shook my head.

"I think you've been set up. I think we've both been set up. I went to the parchment, picked up the quill, and gestured Owen over. "Come, I'll try to get the parchment to show me the words from before."

When Owen stood beside me, I touched the quill to the parchment and said, "Show me the message from before."

As if the parchment understood what I was asking, the paragraph I was talking about came up where it would've been in the message. The rest of the message was blank.

Besides struggling with financial concerns, I have suffered great loneliness during my service as the Legacy Wizard. I do not wish that upon you. I have planted the seeds of companionship for you. However, no one, not even a wizard as powerful as us, has the power to force someone to love another.

"I think you're the seeds," I said, and when I glanced at Owen, I noticed he was pale. "Are you okay?" I asked.

He swallowed hard, then nodded. "I-I'm not ready to marry you or be a companion. I mean, I like you, but you know, we've not even had sex. I-I just... This is a lot."

"Wait, don't freak out yet. Even the old wizard admitted no one can force you to love me or anyone for that matter. I think the old man wanted there to be companionship. Come back downstairs. Orville," I called, and the ghost appeared.

"Your former employer seems to have a sense of humor and had all Owen's belongings sent here and, of course, rented his apartment to someone else. I don't want him to feel like he has to sleep with me. Is there a space where Owen can have his own room?"

Orville seemed to be thinking, then smiled. "Yes, it's a room that's not been used for a long time. It's also rather small, but it's a safe room where the original owner's children would play. Come, I'll show you."

We followed Orville back down to the first floor and into the library. "He bent down and pointed at a copy of C.S. Lewis's *The Lion, the Witch, and the Wardrobe*.

"Please tug that book out," he said to Owen. Owen complied, and when he did, the entire wall slid open.

The room was indeed small and dusty. However, it was bigger than my bedroom in my apartment. Luckily, there was a dusty window in the wall as well. "This has potential, huh?" I asked, and Owen stared at the space.

"It's a secret room off the library," he said, his mouth agape.

"That's a good thing, right?" I asked.

He narrowed his eyes at Orville. "How many ghosts use this room?" he asked.

Orville winked at him. "None that I know of. We prefer a furnished place as much as any other, and as I told you before, we prefer to dwell in the basement. I can ban them from bothering you in this room. However, if I do that, they'll all want to see it, of course."

Owen managed a laugh. "Curiosity doesn't change once we die, it seems."

"Most certainly not. If anything, it makes us more curious. Will this do, Mr. Lloyd?" he asked.

"This is perfect, but it has to be cleaned, and I'll need a bed. Can we do more magic?" Owen asked.

"No," I said, "I think we've exhausted the magic for now. Orville, the bed I had in the attic last night felt new. What happened to it?"

"I don't know, sir. We aren't privy to the knowledge of your predecessor, but I watched him enough to know he could often use what had already been created, even when he needed rest. Maybe if the bed is in the ether, you can just summon it back? Emma," he called, and the ghost appeared before him.

"Can you and Alice clean this room? I will take Mr. Lloyd and Mr. Richards to the kitchen to prepare lunch for them. I'm sure they are rather famished by now."

Her eyes grew large when she saw the room. "Shall I ask cook to prepare something, sir?" she asked without looking away from the hidden space.

"No, cook will be plenty busy in the coming months. For now, I hope sandwiches will do?" he asked, turning toward Owen and me.

Both of us nodded and followed Orville out of the room. He closed the door behind him, and then the music room door closed as well. Apparently, ghosts didn't like to be watched when they cleaned.

Oh well, if it kept me from dusting and cleaning the old space, then so be it. We ate ham and cheese sandwiches while Orville explained how he'd seen the old wizard bring things in and out of the ether. "I understand you will develop a sixth sense, an intuition about your magic, so I would encourage you to do so. If the items already exist, I am sure they aren't disposed of just because of the spells he cast to redecorate the home."

I knew what he was saying was correct. When Emma and Alice appeared, rather dusty and exhausted, I stopped and stared at them. "Listen, I want you to know how much I appreciate you. You too, Orville. You don't owe me anything, certainly not cleaning my home, but thank you for your willingness, especially with Owen being tricked into moving here."

Both women smiled, then looked down. "Thank you, sir," they said simultaneously and disappeared.

Orville was smiling but quickly hid it when I turned back toward him. "Come, sir, let's go see the space, and then you can try to bring the furniture back that you remember."

Chapter Eighteen

OWEN

I WAS ALL UP in my head. I hadn't meant to move in. I'm not even sure Damian asked, but why would he? I was already here, like it or not.

It's not like I loved my apartment. It was small, musty, and often smelled like a dead mouse, but it was all I'd been able to afford. Now, I was in a mansion, and my bedroom, although Orville had called it small, was anything but. I mean, yeah, compared to the rest of the house, it was small, but compared to my dinky apartment, it was gigantic.

I looked over as the two female spirits came in, signaling they'd finished cleaning, and my heart clicked a bit more when Damian thanked them for cleaning the room. I wondered if the old wizard from before had done that too. The smile and blush on their faces made me think probably not.

Damian earned some respect from me for that. "Treat everyone like a CEO, be that the janitor or the boss himself, and you'll go far," my grandfather had told me throughout my childhood.

Apparently, that applied to ghosts too.

The room was spotless when we pulled the CS Lewis book again and peered inside the room. Even the window appeared brand new. I needed to figure out what ghosts liked and get a gift for Emma and Alice as a thank-you.

"Last night," Damian told me, "I slept on a really comfortable bed. I'm going to try to bring it back along with some of the furniture I remember from the room. If you hate it, we can redecorate it when my magic energies level out again. Is that okay?" he asked, and of course, I nodded.

He closed his eyes, and I saw his body blur slightly. When I glanced around, the small room was full of furniture. The twin bed sat on the far wall, away from the window. There was an old chest of drawers and an armoire that would've made C.S. Lewis proud his book had been used to gain entry. It sat on the wall next to the entrance.

I walked to the armoire, and when I saw my clothes, I smiled. "Thank you, Damian. I feel much better with this setup. At least for now."

Damian just smiled. "I gave you blinds for the window. Again, we can work on style tomorrow, and if you want, we can go shopping...you know, the traditional way."

I looked around the room and already knew what I wanted where. "I think I have what I need," I admitted. I stepped into the library and found the books I kept by my bed all the time.

Stuff from my apartment had come into this room as well, including books my dad had read to me before he ran off. It was the one happy memory I still had of him.

I moved a few other things around. Those I hadn't noticed before including my old trumpet from eighth grade. I was never very good, but because of being in the band, I had my first boyfriend. So the trumpet always signified coming out, and more importantly, the love my mom and grandpa had encircled me with when I did.

The last item I moved was the silly old unicorn. I was delighted all the stuffed animals were gone, but I'd missed the little bronze statue the moment I'd given it away. Having it back was a treasure. I placed it on a little table next to the secret door so I could see it no matter where I was in the room.

When I was done, Damian, who'd been sitting in the music room chair playing on his phone while I did my decorating, came over and checked it out. "Oh, man, this is nice, and yeah, like upstairs, this is you."

"Yeah, it does, and thanks for being so cool. I know you didn't mean to have a roommate."

"I don't know if I want to call you that yet or not. So, we should talk, you know. I like you, and I'd love to get to know you–romantically, not just as friends or roommates."

"Friends with benefits?" I teased, and Damian cocked an eyebrow.

"Benefits, for sure, but only when you're ready."

I leaned over to kiss him, and my stomach let out a loud rumble, making us laugh. "Okay, maybe I worked up an appetite, and sandwiches and half a muffin weren't enough. Come on, I'll treat you tonight, and you can tell me how much you're going to charge me to live here." I said.

"Nothing," Damian said without hesitation. "I inherited all of this. I didn't have anything, but now I have millions in the bank and a house worth goodness knows what. No, you're here for free, same as me."

"Well, shit. Then I'm definitely taking you out to dinner." I said, and Damian laughed. I wasn't raised to be a freeloader, so he'd be getting over the idea I wouldn't be paying, but there was no reason to argue now. We could come to terms with that later. For now, I was famished. I'd seen a seafood place on the way over here this morning, and I was chomping at the bit to try it out.

Chapter Nineteen

DAMIAN

T HE WEEK PASSED MUCH quicker than I imagined. Owen and I had some epic make-out sessions, but the whole living together was clearly freaking him out. I mean, I understood, but damn, I really wanted to do things with that sexy little body of his.

I was beginning to get bored, especially since Mr. Stages, Owen's boss, told me I was putting myself at risk of liability by driving and suggested I no longer do that professionally. "You have a significant portfolio, and we've not secured it from liability yet. I recommend you find ways to entertain yourself," he'd said.

Of course, my mind went to his employee and all the ways I could entertain myself with him. I was moping about being lonely. I'm guessing because I looked as bored as I was, Orville, who I'm surprised to say I was getting used to seeing, told me I should begin my training.

At first, I had no idea what he was referring to. I'd forgotten the message on the parchment. I was supposed to use the advice from the parchment to train.

I didn't hesitate to pull it out and place it on the old desk that hadn't been replaced in my magical redecorating.

The moment I touched the quill to the parchment, words began to form.

Excellent, you're ready to get started.

"Yes," I replied. "Can you hear me, or do I have to write?"

I can hear you perfectly fine. Okay, let's get started. First, you should allow my words to transfer to speech.

"Okay. How do I do that?" I asked.

The parchment took me through about an hour of instruction before I was finally able to do the spell, or whatever it was I did to make the words form audible speech.

"That took longer than it should've." The words were spoken as they appeared on the parchment.

"Sorry, I'm not really sure how this all works."

"No need to apologize, but you will need to trust your instincts. Have you not tried your powers before now?"

"Um, the house redecorated itself when I was dreaming."

"No, son, that was a spell I left on the home, just as this parchment is a spell my predecessors cast before they passed. Have you not done anything else on your own?"

I thought for a moment, then remembered fixing Owen's nose. "Oh, yeah, I healed Owen's nose after Alice broke it. She slammed the front door in his face," I said, chuckling. Alice was a total sweetheart. Yes, she was a ghost, but she was one of the nicest people anyone could hope to meet. "She still regrets it."

The parchment didn't say anything back right away, which confused me. Finally, it responded.

"Healing is a powerful spell. One some wizards never master. A healing spell, being your first, does give me insight into what kind of wizard you will become. We can discuss that later. Let's begin preparing your most important weapon. Your staff."

For most of the day, the parchment, which I now referred to as Elias since he was actually speaking to me from across the veil, gave me a lecture on the uses of the staff.

"It gives you balance, as a staff would anyone, but your staff is more important than that. It pulls its power from the earth, water, air, and fire first—the four elements. When you use your powers without it, you draw from your own person. When healing, that's necessary, but when battling dark forces, you must draw the power from the four elements, therefore not exhausting your energy reserves."

It was all fascinating information, but I grew weary of the lectures. I felt like I was back in school. One of my high school teachers was obsessed with American history. He would sometimes spend an entire hour talking about it and by the time the bell rang announcing time to switch classes, we were all asleep.

"You've grown quiet. Have I lost you?"

"Um, maybe a bit. It's a lot of information to take in," I admitted.

"Ah, yes, I can get a bit long-winded. Okay, you have my permission to stop me when I ramble. Remember, I can't see you from where I am. Is Orville with you?"

I searched the room but didn't see the ghost. "No, I don't believe so."

"Ah, you are in the attic room, are you not?"

"I am," I confirmed.

"I should've specified earlier that you should only use the parchment in the attic room. There are wards that can't be breached there. It required too much power to create those levels of wards around the entire home, but the attic was doable. The parchment will attract dark energy, some very nasty dark energy. With its link to the veil, it could possibly open a way for those entities in the world. You should understand these entities are hell-bent on conquering the light and all that is good."

I remembered the man who'd stood threateningly across from the deli the day Owen's boss had given me the parchment and quill. He'd even communicated with me without being close or speaking. The threat was very clear.

"I think I might have already met one of them. It was the day I received the parchment and quill."

"That's too bad. If you've already been spotted, the time before you're forced to battle may be shorter than I'd hoped."

"So, when do I create this staff?" I asked, feeling as if we might need to move this conversation along.

"Ah, I understand why you'd want to proceed, but unfortunately, the staff chooses you, not the other way around. You will call it to you, as my staff was called to me, and the wizards called all their staffs before us. If you're lucky, it comes to you before a need arises. There was a rumor that one wizard centuries ago didn't receive his until he was old. There should be a star painted in the middle of the floor. Can you see it?"

I searched around the room, and finally, I saw it. "I think I see it. Is it gold?"

"Yes. Sit in the middle of the star. Let me know when you're there."

I did as he asked.

"Now, close your eyes and visualize a staff. It doesn't matter if you know what it should look like or not. You can just imagine a stick if you wish. The staff will manifest itself and be what it chooses to be."

I closed my eyes, and at first, the only thing I could visualize was a wand from childhood memories of playing with my friends and I as witches and wizards. Then I forced my mind to remember what I could from *Lord of the Rings* and Gandolf's staff.

"Once you have an image, hold it in your mind. Let it sit there. Don't try to force it; just let it be."

My stomach felt queasy, and with my eyes closed, I felt the room spinning. The image in my mind shifted from a wooden stick with a knob on top, all I had remembered about Gandolf's staff, to one of ornate gold. *Pure gold*, I thought as the image created itself in my mind.

Titanium rings began to wind themselves around the gold exterior. I only knew because I had a passenger who used to be a blacksmith. I'd drive him from downtown to Eugene to visit his mother in a nursing home, then wait for him and take him back to Seattle. It paid well, but it was a long trip.

When metals mix, they're called alloys, and this guy made titanium and gold alloys for dental offices.

As I watched the two metals combine, it became clear that was what was happening. Titanium and gold were both worth a ton of money. Surely, this wouldn't be my staff?

I continued to watch and could hear Elias in the background, but I couldn't make out what he was saying. I was mesmerized by the visions in my mind.

Finally, the metalwork was complete. I felt my right hand, my dominant hand, tingle, and then watched as the staff modified itself so my handprint formed on the side. I instinctively knew it would give me a place to hold the staff comfortably.

Then, to my surprise, different types of wood came from all directions. I recognized weird purple wood from the Amazon, although I couldn't remember its name. Then ebony from Africa, oak, and redwood from here. The wood encircled the staff and formed what appeared to be a flame on top.

As I watched, a light formed inside the wooden flame. It burned brightly but didn't burn the wood. A simple crystal orb sat inside the flame when the light faded.

"Cool," I said. The staff must have heard my voice, although I have no idea why I knew that, because I felt myself rise off the floor and float slightly above the ground.

I could hear Elias now.

"Damian, what's happening? Damian, are you okay?"

I cleared my throat, which was raw, like I'd been screaming for hours. "Um, yeah, and my staff found me."

I couldn't see or hear Elias's reactions, but I could feel him. If he'd been in front of me, I think he would've gasped. There was another long pause.

"Damian, I don't know of any time in history that a wizard was given his staff before months but, usually, years of training."

My body was beginning to ache as if I'd gotten the flu or something. I took the staff to a chair behind the desk and in front of the parchment.

"Um, but that's a good thing, right?" I asked.

"No, I assume it means you will face a nasty foe soon. How are you feeling?"

A cold sweat had developed on my brow.

"Not so good," I admitted.

"Call Orville before you pass out. I must instruct him how to treat you."

Orville appeared, and using my newly honed staff, I did the spell Elias told me to do to give Orville access to hear him through the parchment.

"Damian was nowhere near ready for that level of magic. He will be extremely depleted. He needs round-the-clock care and treatment. Damian, are you able to get to your bed?"

I shook my head. "No, I don't think so."

The last thing I heard was Elias instructing Orville to get me to my bed and then something about making teas or...? Then the world went black.

Chapter Twenty

OWEN

I FELT A QUIVER just over my heart, and then fear spread throughout my body. "Something's wrong," I said out loud.

I'd just finished a meeting with my bosses and a new real estate client and was about to write up my handwritten notes to send to the partners. Cary entered the room and stared at me. "Owen, you don't look so good."

I nodded. "Yeah, something just came over me. I-I think I'm going to take this home and work on it there," I said and stood quickly, grabbing the files I needed to work on and rushing out of the office toward the door.

Cary stopped me. "Owen, be careful," he said cryptically, then shook his head like he'd said something he wasn't supposed to. "You, um, you seem a little pale. Let's get you a taxi."

I knew that wasn't what he was thinking, or at least I thought I knew, but with all the magic bizarreness in my life right now, I wasn't sure I didn't just think everything was weird. I opened my app and ordered a cab because Cary wasn't wrong. I wasn't feeling okay. Something was wrong with Damian. I knew it—not sure exactly how, but I knew.

I was surprised when Cary walked outside with me. The taxi hadn't arrived yet. "Um, I'll be okay," I told him, but he shook his head.

"I'll wait with you," he said.

I didn't argue, mainly because it would do no good, not when I felt so much anxiety. The taxi pulled up, and when I saw the driver, I gasped.

"Nope, we'll pass," Cary said, and the driver seemed to grow in size, which looked extra weird since he was sitting in the driver's seat.

Cary chanted something I couldn't quite make out, and a light flew through the air and struck the driver in the chest.

I closed my eyes because the light that erupted from him was so bright. But when I opened them, stars filled my vision, and the car and the driver were gone.

"I think I'd better drive you myself," Cary said.

"Um, explain what just happened first," I said, and Cary laughed.

"Owen, you are living in an enchanted mansion, given to your wizard man by his wizard predecessor, who hired your magical law firm to handle his will. Do I really need to explain things to you?"

I swallowed hard. "I guess not if you're going to put it that way."

Cary laughed again. "Okay, so you had a premonition. I could tell by how you were acting. Come with me, and I'll drive you home. Can you tell me what you felt?"

I followed him to his car without responding to his question. I didn't know if I could trust Cary, but then, the wizard had met him. Damian's predecessor surely would've known if he could be trusted.

"Um, Cary, did you meet the old wizard? The one with the will?" I asked once we were in his car.

Cary nodded. "Yes, and I hoped maybe I'd be Damian's companion. It would've been quite the thing, a witch and a wizard, not to mention the fact that your wizard man is very attractive."

"Oh, are you mad? Um, jealous?" I asked, surprised.

Cary just laughed. "Do you know how strange it would've been for a Legacy Wizard to mate with a witch? It's a small miracle your wizard is open to a mate in general. My coven holds historical records that go back centuries. The Legacy Wizards have never taken a mate in the past, as far as we know, at least."

"I'm so confused. Why...? No, I'm not mated to Damian. We've only kissed a few times."

Cary leaned back and laughed. "Mating isn't about sex, although if you're lucky, that's a part of it. No, mating is about connection, living with, and spending a lifetime together. Sex?

That's a bonus, of course, especially as hunky as the two of you are."

I shook my head. I'd just learned Cary was a witch of some kind, and to be honest, any other time in my life that would've shocked the shit out of me. Too much had happened though, and clearly, Cary was still as himself as he always was. "Okay, so I've got a lot to catch up on, but, yes, I need to get home soon. I think something's wrong with Damian."

"We're here, honey," Cary said, and I peered out to see we were indeed sitting in front of our house.

"How?" I asked, and Cary just laughed.

"Witch, baby. Why be a witch if you can't manipulate time and space?"

I shook my head. "Okay, I'm going to leave it at that. Do you want to come in?" I asked.

Cary laughed again. "That house will not let me in. Your man will have to okay it, but yes, eventually, maybe, but let's save that for later. Go tend to your man."

I reached over and squeezed Cary's hand. "You need to tell me about that dude you blasted, but yeah, going in now. Thank you, Cary!" I said as I got out of the car and rushed into the house, thankful the gate was still unlocked.

"Orville," I called, but he didn't come. Instead, Emma showed up.

"Oh, Owen, we're so happy you're here. Orville said to send you up to the attic when you got home."

"What's wrong? Is Damian okay?"

She shook her head. "I don't know, but I think something happened. Go on up. Hurry. Poor Damian," she said, and I didn't wait to hear more. I threw my paperwork on a side table and took the steps two at a time, then rushed up the stairs into the attic.

I immediately spotted Damian lying on the bed and rushed toward him. Orville was standing close by, and I could tell he was upset. "Orville, what happened?" I asked.

"Thank the souls you've come home. He exhausted his powers dangerously. He shouldn't have been able to cast a spell like that. Elias... Never mind the details. Elias told me to give you this tea to drink. I've already given the required amount to Damian.

"Owen, he must draw from your life force. It won't hurt. I've seen Elias do it in the past with his...well, his acquaintances. But drink. Hurry."

I didn't ask questions, because I could see how weak Damian was. I took the cup from the table and drank, ignoring the leaves and stuff that hadn't been filtered out.

My head began to spin, and I lay down next to Damian as energy began to flow out of me and into him.

I reached over and took his unconscious hand and wondered why I wasn't more afraid of literally seeing my energy flow into him. "I hope this helps," I said, before falling asleep beside him.

CHAPTER TWENTY-ONE

DAMIAN

I WOKE WITH A raging hard-on and sat up in bed to see Owen asleep, fully clothed, next to me. I quickly scanned the room to see if we were alone, and when there was no sign of Orville, I leaned over and gently kissed Owen on the mouth.

"Mmm," he moaned and stretched before opening his eyes.

"Hi, handsome," I said when he smiled at me.

"You better?" he asked, and I nodded, resisting the urge to ravage him.

He glanced down at the tent in my pants, and when I glanced at him, I saw the same. "I think we both woke, um, wanting?" I said but waited for his permission before I reached out to touch him.

Owen's smile grew, and he reached up and touched my face. "Wanna help me with that?" he asked, gesturing toward his cock with a look.

"Oh, yeah, I really do," I said and immediately took his lips with mine.

Owen jumped up, and quickly took off his suit, barely giving himself enough time to drape it over a nearby chair before leaping back into bed and on top of me.

I ground my naked cock into his, causing him to moan the sexiest moan I'd ever heard.

I chuckled and began kissing down his body, not stopping until I reached his cock.

I glanced up before taking him into my mouth, and we made eye contact. I sucked him in and savored his taste.

"Oh, God, Damian," he all but yelled.

Pleasure flowed through my veins as I took my time devouring his delicious cock, moving up and down his length and edging him closer and closer to completion.

"God," he said before bucking into my mouth again.

To save me from ending this sooner than I wanted, I forced myself to stop, knowing he was too close to coming for me to continue. His smile was wicked as I reached his face after I'd kissed and nipped my way back up his body, enjoying the taste and feel of him under me. When we were face-to-face, I slowly moved my body down his, letting my sac glide down him until his cock slid between my balls and ass.

"Fuck, you're hot," he said as I moved my hands over his muscular body. He fucked against my taint, sending pleasure shooting through me as I leaned over and savored the flavor of his mouth.

His aroma, a mixture of cologne and soap, heightened my senses, arousing me like some pheromone.

He surprised me then by pushing me back and throwing his legs up and around me before positioning his ass against my cock. I groaned with delight as my cock bounced against his hole.

"God, I want you so much," I said and would've pressed down, taking him dry, had he not stopped me.

"Got a condom? Or do you use PReP?" he asked. I nodded, suddenly feeling shy.

"PReP," I managed to whisper, then waved my hand, and a bottle of lube appeared.

He laughed as he took it from me and lubed his ass and my cock at the same time. God, this man was good, so fucking deliciously good. I cried out with pleasure as he slowly slid my cock inside him.

"God, oh God," he moaned as the head entered him. Unable to stop myself, his ass feeling so fucking amazing encircling my cock, I thrust gently as my brain scrambled.

"Oh, fuck, yeah, yeah!" I yelled. My words seemed to encourage him as he worked my cock the rest of the way in. "Oh, God!" I cried again when his balls hit my ass.

"More!" he demanded. I fucked him as hard as I could from that position, then lifted him off me. He immediately got onto all fours, and I lined myself up behind him, amazed at how well our bodies fit together.

My nerve endings burst into fire as I fucked him harder and harder into the mattress, him yelling sensual encouragements as I did.

I wanted to see his face, so I pulled out, leaned over him, and asked him to lie on his back. He quickly did as I asked, and when I entered him again, my heart did a strange little fluttering thing. *Magic—this is fucking magic*, I thought as our eyes locked.

I leaned in and kissed him, still fucking him. I must've hit his prostate because when I pulled back from the kiss, he moaned, "Fuck! Oh, fuck! Harder, Damian. Fuck me harder!" I did as he asked, thrusting inside him, over and over, until I was seconds away from coming.

No sooner had the sensation hit me than his cum burst out of him, coating us both.

My orgasm hit me before he'd finished, and I emptied into his gorgeous ass. I admit it, I've got a bizarre cum kink, and seeing Owen covered in so much of his spunk sent me into ecstasy. I pulled out, leaned over, and licked it up.

I would've swallowed, but Owen's face showed desire, and I instantly knew he was into the same kink as me. I leaned over and let his come drip from my mouth into his before the two of us kissed and swallowed the product of our lovemaking.

"Fuck," I said as I fell to his side. "That was too fucking hot."

After a long time of pure postsexual bliss with Owen lying next to me, I got up, went to the bathroom, and grabbed a towel to clean us both up.

I paused in the doorway as I was headed back, gazing at Owen's still naked body in my bed. "That was... You were amazing," I said, causing him to laugh.

"You assessing my fucking skills, wizard?" he asked, and I laughed out loud.

"Cocky much?" I asked as I went over and pinned him to the bed.

He pressed his spent cock against me, teasing me. I rolled off and watched him for several more seconds before grabbing the towel and washing him off, then tucking it under his ass to catch what I'd left there. "I really like you," I admitted and felt odd confessing my feelings this early in the game. I certainly wasn't used to that, since I usually only hooked up, but Owen was so much more than a hookup. I needed to come to terms with that.

He didn't respond, just rolled over and kissed me. "Gotta get a shower; then I'm starving, so let's go see what's in the kitchen."

He was already in the bathroom before I could respond, so I rolled over onto my back. The sex had been amazing, and we'd both been so freaking horny. Much hornier than I'd ever been before. At least, speaking for myself. I'd never needed a release that hard. I wouldn't be surprised if my cum hadn't bruised his internal organs. Not that he hadn't come just as hard as I had.

The last thing I remembered before waking next to Owen was passing out after I'd created the staff.

"The staff," I said out loud and jumped up, looking for it. I searched around the room where I'd passed out, and then, in a panic, I called Orville.

He showed up with a smile spread across his face. "Um, I take it you learned the side effect of waking up after absorbing energy from a partner," he said, and I immediately blushed, forgetting I was still naked.

"Um, did you put the staff somewhere?" I asked.

He shook his head. "No, but it is with you. I don't know where it goes, but I saw it appear a few times when Elias needed his. Try holding out your right hand and imagining it there."

I did as he instructed, and he was right. The staff was in my hand, looking as beautiful as it had in my imagination. "Wow," I heard behind me and saw Owen coming out of the bathroom, a towel wrapped around him. "What's that?" he asked.

He nodded slightly at Orville, acknowledging his presence, then cocked an eyebrow at me, clearly referring to me being naked in the ghost's presence.

"I-I made this," I said.

"That's why he was in such need of your help," Orville replied. "I'm not a wizard, nor have I ever had powers, but even I know the staff took too much of his life force to create. It's unwise to use that much, no matter how powerful you are. I don't recommend you do that again."

I nodded, knowing what he said was correct. "I didn't know what I was doing," I said.

"You need to work with Elias and your parchment to figure that out. Had it not been for Owen, I'm not sure how we would've helped you recover."

"How did Elias deal with it?" I asked, and Orville shrugged.

"I don't know. I didn't meet Elias until he was well within his powers. He came to live here after my last employer died. With Elias's help, I was able to manifest, so I'm not sure how he dealt with his mistakes, his growing pains, before he arrived."

I went to the parchment. At that point, both Orville and Owen had seen me naked, so I wasn't in any hurry to shower, and I used the quill to open the communication with Elias. He responded immediately.

"Did you recover okay?"

"Yes, thanks to Orville and Owen," I said, turning to see a confused-looking Owen.

"Hold on. I'm going to make it so Owen can hear," I said, then quickly did the same spell I'd done earlier. This time, however, the staff appeared, and I felt the power come from it rather than from me. "Cool," I said, causing Orville to chuckle. Luckily, with the staff's help, it went much faster than it had with Orville.

"Elias, meet Owen. Owen, this is my predecessor, Elias."

"Hello, Owen, I'm very pleased to meet you."

"Um, thanks, sir," Owen said. "The pleasure is mine."

"Elias, what happened? I felt like I was dying earlier."

"The staff took too much of your life force. You almost did die, or at least would have gone into a coma. You were lucky Orville had experienced similar situations before."

"So, is this something that can happen again?" Owen asked. "If so, how do we prevent it from hurting him?"

Elias took a moment to think.

"I kept the tea with me at all times. It's simple to make, and Orville has the recipe, although I doubt he knew why he was making it. However, if you're ever in a situation like that again, you can drink the tea, and if someone is close to you and willing to give their life force for you, they can help you recover. They simply need to drink the tea, and it'll happen automatically."

"Is it dangerous? Could it hurt or kill the other person?" I asked.

"No, the spell prevents the other person from being harmed. It can't take more life force than they can handle, but you will both be tired or need some way to rebuild your forces."

"Like sex?" Owen asked.

We couldn't hear the sounds Elias made, but when he responded, it was clear he was laughing. Or at least I assumed he was.

"Yes, sex is a powerful tool for rebuilding your life force."

"Fun too," I said, and Owen snorted behind me.

"Um, Elias, sir, if I drink the tea, and Damian is in danger or passed out like he was this time, does it still work? Or does he have to have it, or...well, Orville gave it to me earlier."

"The tea is enchanted, at least when made in the attic space. The spell I cast long ago there will remain in effect as long as the attic exists. So, you can make the tea, or Orville can make it for you. Then you can carry it on your person. But both Damian and you *must* drink it before it'll work. If he is unconscious, pour a drop into his mouth. Even a drop will work."

"Good to know. Thank you, sir."

I turned toward Owen, who appeared perplexed, if not concerned about everything. I went over and hugged him. "It's okay. I'm sure we'll be okay."

"Owen, since Damian has decided to share our connection with you, I would like to educate you on a few things you should prepare for. Legacy wizards are warriors—soldiers for the light and all things good. We serve the light while keeping the balance, which means we must allow some dark to permeate the world. As long as innocents are not harmed, we don't stop the dark because doing so would create an imbalance. I share this with you because Damian knows this innately, but you are something new—an experiment. The dark wants more power. They push to upset the natural balance on our planet. In space, darkness controls all, yet there are forces, such as the sun, that shed light in the dark. The stars themselves are evidence that light exists throughout the universe.

When the dark forces come for Damian; they will use everything at their disposal to fight him. That puts you at extreme risk. I have created tools to help you and called upon servants of the light to assist you in times of need. However, and this is for both you and Damian, if you find this too much for you, don't be embarrassed to step away. You have special qualities, or you would never have been attracted to Damian, and vice versa. However, it is unlikely that you are a wizard or a witch. I have to assume you are simply of the light, a torch that burns in the night. I doubt it was never your destiny to fight the dark forces, simply to be that torch."

"Is his life at risk?" I quickly asked.

"No more than any other innocent on Earth. However, the dark will try to use him to manipulate you, as it will all your friends and relations. Nothing is sacred to the forces who work against you. Keep your eyes open, Owen, and if ever you feel you are in danger, you should be able to call upon the light to help you. Sometimes that may be Damian, but it could also be other guardians of the light. Don't fear the darkness that gives them power, but call upon the guardians when you need help."

"You said the dark will attack my friends? Are they in danger?" I asked, fearing for Molly all of a sudden.

"The guardians are all around you, Damian. Even when you can't see them, they are there. If an innocent is taken or about to be harmed in any way, they will protect them. However, if your friends or even you, Owen, choose the dark or use the darkness for personal gain, there is little the guardians will do to save you. Even Damian's powers are limited when it comes to helping a darkling.

"What...a darkling?" I asked, but even as I did, I knew instinctively that he meant anyone who used dark energy to get what they wanted. Sure enough, Elias confirmed that to Owen.

"So, the rule is don't use dark energy. I'm beginning to get an image of what that means, so I'll share that with Owen," I said as a list of dark things filled my mind. It wasn't stuff that we didn't understand. Aggression for the sake of aggression, murder, lies, greed, the biblical seven deadly sins, for example, minus gluttony. Interesting that was left out.

I got dressed while Owen asked more questions. I realized I already knew the answer to some, but I liked that he had access to my mentor. That's what I saw Elias as, via his parchment and quill. Owen was some sort of experiment. That was strange to me. It also concerned me. I would wait until it was just Elias and me to learn more about that, but for now, I knew I needed to protect him, and I didn't trust Elias had done everything he could.

CHAPTER TWENTY-TWO

OWEN

THE KITCHEN SMELLED AMAZING when we came down the stairs. "What's that?" I asked.

"That would be cook," Alice said as she floated out of the wall toward the kitchen.

"Cook?" I asked, but Alice had already disappeared again. I would never get used to that.

Orville appeared in front of us seeming perturbed. "I apologize before we even go into the kitchen. Cook is, let's just say Cook is a force unto themselves. None of us, not even I, have ever seen them. They come when they wish, and they leave the exact same way. Never, and I mean this with the direst of dire warnings, ever criticize the food. If you don't like it, simply leave it on your plate. Compliments are fine, although I'm not entirely certain cook cares if you like their cooking or not."

We came around the staircase, and my mouth fell open at the spread. Homemade bread? That's the first thing I saw, and being a total carbaholic, that's the thing that made my mouth water first. Then I scanned the rest of the food, noting a leg of lamb and mashed potatoes.

"Oh my God, is that a freshly baked cheesecake? Strawberry cheesecake?" I asked, and Orville snickered behind me.

"Wait, what's all this for?" I asked. "It's just two of us."

"Hardly," Orville added, and I turned toward him.

"Do ghosts eat?" I asked.

He laughed. "No, we don't have bodies, but we do eat in a way. We still have the ability to taste, but it's not food in this dimension." He paused and shook his head. "There are way too many elements of that to explain when there's warm food waiting for you. Go, sit in the dining room, and we'll serve you."

"Orville, there's no need. We can serve ourselves."

"Definitely not. We love what we do, and most of us miss it, so please, Owen, allow us to do this."

I shrugged, took Damian's hand, and went into the beautiful open kitchen dining room combo that had been created. Emma and Alice both showed up and began plating our food. I thanked them both when Alice poured wine and Emma fixed a plate and placed it in front of me.

Orville stood next to the parlor door, his hands behind his back. "Orville," I said, "you were telling me what happens with the food."

He cocked an eyebrow and sighed. "This generation has no decorum. When in Rome..." he said, rolling his eyes. He came over and sat next to me.

"There are millions of entities that exist within the living planes. I don't know exactly how many, nor have I ever seen them all. I just know because Elias has told me so. The food was left out when we were done eating, and Elias summoned them. I don't know how. I assume that's something you will do, Damian," he said, looking at him. "Regardless, we can't see what's happening, only that the food disappears, and all the plates are spotlessly clean. And I assure you cook has no tolerance for things not spotless, so if their cleaning meets their approval..."

Despite his ominous warnings regarding cook, I could tell Orville had an affinity for them. Remembering the decorum comment, I turned to Orville and asked if there were rules he wanted us to follow regarding the meal.

"When in Rome," he repeated but smiled at me. "No, just try not to drop food down your front, and please eat with your mouth closed. The rest we can tolerate."

"You sound like my mom," I said, chuckling.

"Someone should," Orville said, and I laughed.

I looked over at Damian, who was also smiling, then I reached over, took his hand, and squeezed before I took my first bite.

Of course, the bread was what I went for first, smearing it with the butter Emma had placed on the table. "Oh my God!"

I said, my mouth full, then cringed when I saw Orville cock an eyebrow.

I quickly swallowed. "I'm sorry, Orville, but you didn't tell me the food would be like this. It's... Damn, this is the best food I've ever had."

Orville swallowed and turned his gaze toward the kitchen. "Um, cook isn't a fan of profanity. Sorry, I should've warned you. Although in my day, profanity was avoided in most situations."

I bit into the heavenly bread again, and this time, I chewed slowly, letting the incredible yeasty flavor fill my palate. When I swallowed, I nodded toward Orville. "No profanity, got it.

"Cook," I said to the room. "You cook like this, and you can boss me around all you want."

Emma chuckled behind me, and I turned to wink at her. "You might be cautious telling that to any ghost, because we all tend to be bossy."

"Sorry, I only offer that to cook 'cause they're the king or queen of this castle, let me tell you. Jeez, this is amazing."

Even Orville smiled, then stood and went back to his perch by the parlor door.

Damian didn't respond as much as I did, but I loved food more than I should. Was I a foodie? Nah, that was too pompous for the likes of me. My mother was a restaurant critic before she became a judge, but unlike her, I didn't want to critique someone's cooking. I just wanted to eat it.

I was almost too full to eat the cheesecake, but I forced myself to stop eating in time for at least a small bite.

"Oh, God in heaven, this is divine. Cook, I'm in love with you," I called out, and this time, I swear I heard laughter from somewhere in the kitchen. I had a feeling cook and I were about to become best friends. Or at least on my side.

"Orville, I may need you to roll me to the library," I said as I leaned back, patting my stomach. "That has to be the best meal I've ever eaten."

Damian stood and came around the table, pulling me up from my seat and kissing me. "Come on, all that moaning and groaning has me hungry for more of you," he said, and I laughed as I followed him up the stairs.

"You know, ain't nothing happening when I'm this full, right?"

"I know. I'm supposed to be a wizard and will be trying to cure that with my magical powers," he said, causing me to laugh.

"Hey, eating like that followed by more sex with a sexy wizard? Yeah, count me in!"

Chapter Twenty-Three

DAMIAN

O WEN HAD TO GO in early to work the next day to catch up on everything he missed by coming home to rescue me from the "staff incident," as I was now calling it.

I spent the day as I had the day before, allowing Elias to instruct me. I teased him a few times about how I felt like he was training me to be a boxer since we spent three hours focusing on where my feet were when I drew the staff.

"You can lose your balance if your feet aren't planted firmly," Elias instructed more than once.

Doing magic? Really, that didn't feel all that strange now either. The staff came and went when I called it. Ghosts popped in and out of my life all the time. These things were par for the course.

It seemed like so much time had passed since it all started, since I'd walked into that magic shop and the weird man had given me the Wheel of Fortune card.

Funny I should think of that, but now I was thinking about all the symbols on it. The wheel turned, of course, but there was dark and light. Life had turned for me, but I also figured I'd been thrown in the middle of that wheel.

The real question was, what would happen when it turned again?

Chapter Twenty-Four

OWEN

I CLOSED THE DOOR and pointed toward the chair at the side of my desk. "Okay, explain. You're a witch?" I asked.

Cary laughed. "Obviously, and so are Mr. Stages and Mr. Harrison. In fact, so is Lemmie Sue," Cary said, referring to our legal assistant, Mrs. Patterson. Although the name sorta worked as the woman was always talking about who should sue whom.

"Okay, so why me? Why did I get hired?" I asked.

Cary shrugged. "I don't know. You'll have to ask the partners, but I assume it's because of the light that shines from you. You've always been almost a little too bright to look at."

"What's that supposed to mean?" I asked and threw a paper wad at him.

"You are what we say in the business, a Goody Two-shoes."

"Is that what they say?"

"Yep, and you're one of the biggest."

"Why? 'Cause I don't murder people?"

"You don't, nor do you disparage anyone. You are always kind and offer a smile even when you're sad or frustrated or don't want to do something I stuck on your desk just to get you riled up."

"Ugh, do not tell me you've been giving me extra work to see how long it'd take to yell at you."

Cary put his hands up and laughed. "I didn't admit to anything, but you are a straight shooter," he said, and this time, I laughed loud enough that he stiffened and glanced toward the door, probably to make sure our bosses weren't coming to yell at us.

"There's nothing straight about me, Cary, or you for that matter. Okay, so I now know there are light guardians, and from the weird blasting thing you did with the scary taxi man, I assume you are one of them."

He nodded. "We all are," he admitted.

"I'm not. I'm just a torch or something like that."

Cary cocked his head and looked at me before answering. "Do you know what a torch does?" I shook my head. "Have you ever been in a cave? Deep below the earth when someone turned off the light?" he asked, and I remembered the trip my grandfather, Mom, and I took to Mammoth Cave National Park when I was still in high school. The tour guide had done just that, and the darkness was so intense it almost felt liquid.

"Yeah," I answered.

"When the light came back on, what happened?" he asked.

"I don't know. The room was no longer dark."

"Did it feel like the darkness just disappeared or did it feel like it scurried away?"

I thought about that for a moment, then sighed. "It scurried, didn't it?" I asked.

Cary smiled. "I'm a guardian, not a torch. I don't bring light to the world, but I can use the light. Without torches, people like you, we wouldn't be able to balance the light and darkness. Don't get me wrong, when darkness stays in its place, follows the rules of balance, it brings its own benefits. All animals need the dark to keep their circadian rhythms in place. Plants need the dark to grow and thrive. Winter is necessary for most plants to produce fruit. Don't be too quick to demonize the darkness: any guardian, your boyfriend included, will understand there is no balance without the dark. The light forces however know that dark has always strived to regain its dominance. To return to how things were before the so-called big bang occurred. Guardians need torches to keep that from happening."

"You need the sun," I said and picked up some of the paperwork to begin working. When Cary didn't leave as he usually did when I showed I was ready to get back to work, I looked up.

"You are, in essence, a very tiny, but very powerful ball of solar energy. Never underestimate what you and others like you bring to the table," he said and then rose.

"I don't know what Elias Ericson had in mind when he put you in Damian's path, nor am I sure it is a good idea for a

Legacy Wizard to be mated. Many guardians continue to argue that point, but I do know he is very lucky to have you, as am I and the partners," he said, glancing up toward where their offices were.

I smiled, got up from my desk, came around, and hugged him. "Thank you, Cary," I said when we pulled back. "Now, if I find out you gave me busy work again, I'm going to figure out how to use that solar power to burn your ass!"

Cary burst out laughing and was still laughing as he left my office.

I sat back once he was gone and pondered what he said. Was I a torch? A little piece of sunlight? I guess, in a way, we were all at least some element of our sun. We certainly couldn't survive without it, at least. I liked the romantic thought of bringing something important to the table.

Was that what light was to magical guardians? I didn't know, but that didn't mean I didn't like it.

That evening, before leaving work, I asked Cary if he thought I was safe to go home on foot, and he paused, then nodded. "I don't feel anything, but if anyone makes you uncomfortable, call your man's name even if you call him in your mind. You could call me or the other guardians, but a Legacy Wizard is the most powerful of all of us. If you have him on speed dial, that's who you should ask for."

I smiled and winked before walking out. I did have the sexy Damian on speed dial, literally. I always craved his arms and his kisses, and damn, I was craving them right now.

Thinking of cravings, hopefully cook was up to their magical ways tonight too.

I could not wait to see what they fixed for us next.

Chapter Twenty-Five

DAMIAN

O WEN AND I WERE sitting in the little deli across from his office when the law firm's receptionist, Cary, came in. The guy had flirted shamelessly with me from the moment I met him, but I got a distinct feeling that was just his character.

Owen didn't seem the least bit surprised or concerned, and I wasn't sure how I felt about that. I mean, I didn't want a jealous boyfriend, but I didn't mind him caring a little.

"So," Owen said, moving nervously and glancing around for listening ears. "I, um, wanted you to meet Cary because he's, you know, on the same team."

"Honey, it's the 2020s. You can say the gay word." I said, chuckling.

Owen rolled his eyes toward Cary, which made him laugh. I'd already clocked him as a witch. My internal voice told me that when he walked into the deli. I didn't understand what that meant, just that he wasn't a threat.

"I think he means the witch thing," Cary said, laughing when Owen looked around. "Baby, nobody cares about that these days either. The ones who hear it just think we're a bunch of nutters. The ones who know, already knew."

"Damian," Cary said and extended his hand. "It's a delight to meet you, on friendlier and less professional terms, that is."

I chuckled and took the witch's hand, pulling back when the little bastard electrocuted me, but his grin gave away the fact that he was just being naughty. He waggled his eyebrows and said, "I've got a very electric personality."

"Cut it out, Cary, or I won't invite you to have lunch with us again," Owen said and stuffed his mouth with a hoagie.

"Ugh, you are no fun, Owen. You get to sleep with the hunky wizard. At the very least, you should let me play with him."

I cocked my eyebrow and wondered if I could somehow zap him back, but my powers immediately shut down the idea. There are a lot of differences between a wizard and a witch. They aren't powerful enough to worry about keeping everything locked down. On the other hand, I apparently had to watch my every move when it came to magic.

As the epiphany came to me, I sighed and, reaching over, took several of Cary's potato chips instead. When he cocked an eyebrow at me, I shrugged. "I can't zap you back, so I decided petty theft would be my revenge."

Cary stared at me for a few seconds and burst out laughing. "Oh, I like you, wizard. Okay, so when are you two tying the knot, and can I be the flower girl?"

The rest of the meal was like that, and secretly, I couldn't wait to get Molly and Cary together. Would I regret that for the rest of my life? Oh yeah, because they were going to be impossible together. Not to mention what would happen if Molly ever figured out that Cary was an actual, honest-to-goodness witch. Ugh, maybe I shouldn't introduce them.

My phone buzzed, and instinctively, I knew it was the devil I'd just been thinking of. "Hey stranger, about time you called me."

"Phones work both ways, butch," she said, using my nickname since she said I wasn't gay acting enough, whatever that meant, to be a bitch.

"Whatever," I replied like I always did. "Where've you been? I want you to have dinner with Owen, me, and maybe even my new friend, Cary."

Cary's eye went up, and I could see mischief pouring out of him. At that moment, he looked a hell of a lot more like an imp than a witch. I'd have to ponder that one a bit.

"I've been so busy with work, but I told my boss that if she didn't pull back, I'd quit, so I've got some time. What about tonight?"

I closed my eyes to see if I could contact Orville in my mind. Of course, I did, which was awesome.

"Orville, would it be possible to bring over guests tonight?"

"Not your seance friends again?" he asked sarcastically.

"One of them, yes, but the other is a witch."

I could feel Orville's alarm.

"Elias never allowed witches in his home."

"Yes, and I feel the alarm bells going off, but this one is a friend of Owens's. I'd like him to feel welcome."

"I can't restrict who you invite, but don't expect him to be welcomed by the other residents."

"Damian," I heard Molly say.

"Yeah, sorry I got distracted. Come by the house tonight. We'll show you the renovations and see what you think. Also if he'll come, I'm inviting our friend. You'll like him; he's a witch."

"Oh, is he single?"

"I think not on your team, even if he is."

Cary laughed across from me as Molly moaned in my ear. "Why can't I meet a nice straight witch? Okay, well, I get off at five and can come over then."

"Five thirty it is."

I closed my eyes again after I hung up and asked Orville if cook planned to prepare a meal tonight or if I needed to grab pizza because I sure didn't want to offend the spirit if it meant they wouldn't cook like that for us again.

"Cook only does what they want to. You should prepare your own meal."

The curt reply made it clear how Orville felt about my having a witch over for dinner.

I opened my eyes, and Cary was staring at me, his mischievous eyes watching my every move. "Okay, well, against my, I don't know what I'd call Orville. My resident ghost?" I said, and Owen choked on his water. I clapped him on the back and kept talking. "I'm inviting you to my home tonight, but they're not real happy. I'd recommend you only go the kitchen/dining combo and the parlor."

"What if I need the powder room?" he asked seriously, and I laughed.

"I think I can convince Orville to allow that."

He nodded. This time, he wasn't smiling. "It's very unusual to receive an invitation to a wizard's home. Much less if you have ghosts in residence. You're new. Are you sure you wish to open that can of worms?"

I searched my thoughts for any instinctual concerns, and although there was certainly a reticence from the ghosts coming at me, I couldn't see any reason why I shouldn't trust Cary. I stared at him for a moment more while weighing all the concerns.

From what I could see, the main one was the same as the movies said about vampires. Once you invited one in, they could come and go as they chose. Of course, the only difference between most homes and ours was that ours was full of spirits that I doubt even a witch could contend with.

"I can see no reason not to invite you in, but the invitation applies only to you, not your coven, not your relations, only you. If I choose to open an invitation to others, it will be done individually. Can you commit to that?" I asked, and Cary nodded, the smile still gone. I felt how important it was to give a consequence, so I sighed and wished I didn't have to come off as rude, but apparently, it was required.

"Know this, witch. If you break this agreement, you will never be allowed in or around my residence again. That includes the entire neighborhood."

"As it should," Cary said and lifted his hand. I did the same, and light transferred between us, sealing the bond and the agreement.

Cary's smile returned as I glanced at Owen, whose mouth was agape. "That was intense."

"Oh, you'll get used to it. When you have the power that your boyfriend has, you have to be very careful about who you invite into your home. I am very honored, wizard, as will all my coven be. You have earned yourself a lot of very useful allies by your generosity."

I snorted. "You say that, but you haven't met our house full of spirits yet."

Cary stopped short. "House *full* of spirits?" he asked.

"Oh, very full. Orville, also a spirit, has yet to tell me how many, but I know it's several dozen."

He shook his head. "You are a very strange wizard, Damian, but more power to you, and I appreciate the warning. I'll wear my citrine pendant, just in case."

I realized that citrine repelled harmful spirits, but I seriously doubted that any crystal would hold off the spirits in my home. Not only because there were a lot of them, but even more importantly, having lived over a century with a powerful wizard, they had also manifested powers, although Orville denied it. I didn't think they were the kind that could be used outside their own forms, but they could and likely would be formidable if provoked.

Chapter Twenty-Six

OWEN

DINNER PARTY, DINNER PARTY. Oh dinner, dinner, dinner. Dinner party. I kept humming the words to the tune of the song "Lollipop" the rest of the afternoon. I almost invited my bosses over, too, when I remembered how serious Cary had become when Damian invited him. It was a big deal to come into a wizard's home. Or was it domain? Maybe I was getting into this whole wizard and witch game now.

Regardless, I loved the home we'd established in such a short time, and I liked Molly. I also couldn't wait to see how Cary and Molly got along. I imagined it would either be amazing or the two would clash like lightning and water.

When Cary refrained, and yes, I realized now that's what this was, from dumping a bunch of paperwork on my desk, I met him out front after the partners left for the day. "Okay, you driving?" I asked.

Cary nodded, then told Mrs. Patterson we were leaving. I followed him to his car and climbed in. "Owen, you do realize how significant it is for him to invite me over? I know he does. He's *the* Legacy Wizard, but do you?"

"I do, I guess. I don't understand why it's such a big deal. Is it because you can now come visit anytime afterward?"

Cary laughed. "Honey, witches are the original Central Intelligence Agency. We can come and go undetected in almost any home, building, business, or other place as long as it's not warded to keep us out. By inviting me to his home, your sweetheart has made the statement that he trusts me implicitly."

"But you wouldn't come into our home uninvited, would you?"

"Not likely. A wizard is a powerful ally and a terrifying enemy. Not to mention, you have resident ghosts. You know how strange that is, don't you?"

"It's strange, but they are pretty awesome when you get to know them. I haven't gone into the basement yet, and I don't recommend anyone do, but the ones who come into our living space are kind and helpful. I sort of think of them as friends."

Cary shook his head. "You're as strange as him. The two of you belong together."

I smiled and winked at him. "I think you're right about that, or that's how it feels."

We chatted all the way to the house, and I showed him the little alcove in front of the fence where he could park and not get a ticket for blocking a sidewalk. Luckily, whoever added the fence likely did so in anticipation of a need for a place for people to park while still protecting the perimeter.

We reached the gate, and Cary stopped just outside. "I'm, it's not open to me," he said.

"Damian," I called quietly so as not to sound like I was yelling at him. He appeared a moment later at the front door and waved his hand when he saw Cary standing there. Cary nodded and stepped through the gate. A bluish light activated around the gate as he walked through. I watched transfixed as that light then radiated around him, before it encompassed the entire property.

Cary winked at me when I turned back toward Damian. "One down, one to go," he said, and we walked toward the front door together. This time, Damian shook Cary's hand but didn't let go. Instead, he pulled him through the door. A *pop* sounded as Cary walked through.

"That one hurt a little," Cary said, rubbing his arms.

"Better safe than sorry. Wouldn't you agree?" Damian asked, and Cary nodded.

"Indee—" He stopped before he got the word out. In front of us stood not just Orville, Alice, and Emma, but four other ghosts I'd never seen before. The other four were huge and slightly obscured from view.

Orville stepped forward, regarding Cary. "Why should we allow you in, witch? What guarantee do we have that you aren't up to no good?"

"Orville," Damian said, but the ghost ignored him.

Cary shook his head and, under his breath, said what sounded like "Ghosts."

He reached up, pulled a necklace off, and handed it to Orville. "This is the only thing I have to demonstrate my intentions."

I'd never seen Orville take something from the living, not me or Damian, but he took the necklace and held it away from him like it was a soiled baby's diaper. He disappeared through the back wall, and several tense moments passed before he returned without the necklace.

"You may stay within this area, the entry, dining room, kitchen, and parlor." He motioned toward the closed door to his right. "And, as Master Damian has requested, the powder room, but know this, you are being watched and will be watched the entire time you are here. If you try anything to harm the residents of this home, we *will* destroy you!"

"Orville," Damian chastised again, but Cary just shook his head. "Your warning is understood. I promise to stay within my boundaries."

I almost expected him to joke about ghosts watching him pee, but he didn't move until all the ghosts dispersed.

"That went better than expected," Cary said.

I didn't expect all the ghosts to leave, but I could feel as much as see they were all gone. Even Orville had left us alone.

"What's that all about?" I asked.

Cary didn't respond, so I looked toward Damian. "I'm just understanding," he said, glancing at Cary. "But let's just say witches and ghosts have a tenuous relationship, and," he said, giving me a very stern eye, "let's leave it at that."

Cary nodded. "At least the parts of your home I can see are lovely. Tell me, who did your design?" he asked and laughed, clearly knowing the décor had happened magically.

Molly showed up shortly after the big standoff, and I was happy she'd missed it. I didn't know her well, but I did know she wanted to understand the magical world more than she did. Too bad she couldn't find out about her best friend being one of the world's most powerful wizards.

Cary and Molly circled each other for about half an hour, but they'd found common ground by the time the pizza arrived. Of course, that common ground was some food truck, tarot card, mystic event thing that apparently drives around Seattle popping up in obscure yet fun areas.

I wondered how Molly would feel to find out Cary really was what she and her friends professed to be. I also wondered how she'd feel knowing the ghosts here thought of her the same way she and Cary did about fake fortune tellers.

I'd never tell; that was for sure. We moved things over to the parlor, which, to be honest, was a little odd since I rarely ever used it. The ghosts tended to keep that part of the house shut off. When Damian spent time down there, and not in his room in the attic, he did so in the music room or library, which, as far as I was concerned, was the most comfortable room in the house, although I probably felt that way because it was mostly my stuff in there.

Damian, when alone, usually hung out in the living room equivalent of the second floor, and I knew when he was there, he wanted to be alone. He didn't even have to tell me. I just understood.

We were getting along perfectly for two people who'd been virtual strangers just a short time ago.

Would that last? I wondered. Damian reached over and squeezed my hand, making my heart fill with happiness. Cary instantly noticed and began making excuses to leave. "Thank you, Damian, and of course, Owen," he said and turned to me, although I knew it was more for Damian's sake, "for inviting me over tonight. I won't forget the honor of it."

Molly seemed perplexed for a moment, then stood. "I'll follow you out. I'll just call for a taxi. Now that my free ride is gone," she said but smiled at Damian.

"Why don't you let me be your taxi bootie call tonight," Cary said, and Molly laughed.

"Ugh, if only you were at least a little straight, that might be offensive. Although tempting," Molly said and laughed as Cary all but pulled her out of the house.

"Bye, honeys," Cary said once he got past the gate.

"Bye-bye," Molly called, and Damian and I stood on the front porch laughing as they left.

When we went back in, the ghosts were still nowhere to be seen. "We should probably go on up. I'm guessing they won't be coming out again tonight."

"Mind explaining why?" I asked. Damian shook his head and led the way up to the attic. Once there, he sat on the chair beside his desk and pulled off his socks.

"I didn't quite get it until Orville and the others confronted Cary. History isn't one of the things my gift shares readily. Apparently, witches and ghosts are bitter enemies. Of course, I didn't know that when I invited Cary over."

"Enemies?" I asked.

"Something to do with an ancient sorcerer. He used spirits to his own end, and the witches, unable to defeat him, began forcing ghosts to cross the veil. That's a practice they still do, even though the old sorcerer was long ago defeated."

"Aah, and ghosts don't necessarily like being forced to move on before they're ready."

"That's what I gathered from my insight."

I stared at him and sighed. "I don't understand all this. It seems so strange sometimes. Do you just know things?"

Damian shrugged. "I do. It was strange at first, but I've learned to just go with the flow. Now, how about going with this flow?" he asked, unbuttoning my shirt.

"Oh yeah, this is the kind of flow I'm all about," I purred.

Chapter Twenty-Seven

DAMIAN

T HE NIGHT WAS GLORIOUS. Owen slept snugly in my arms, and although I didn't sleep, my heart overflowed having him there. Not just that, having had Cary here, as well as Molly, felt right too.

Molly rarely came to my apartment. Mostly because it was in a not-so-great part of town but also because so much of my father had been there, the place never felt like it belonged to me. I think even though my beloved witch-wannabe friend didn't have Cary's powers, she was intuitive enough to feel uncomfortable.

Tonight had been very different. She'd settled in like she'd been coming over for years. I had expected her to gasp about how quickly the rooms had changed. There was no way a renovation like this could occur in such a short time.

What struck me was she didn't even seem to notice. If she had, she would've known magic had to have been involved.

Cary was a totally different turn of events. I hadn't understood the significance of him coming over until he walked through the wards. That's when the alarms went off in my head. Witches are primarily guardians of the light but could change alliances easily enough.

Cary was, of course, no threat to me now or likely ever. He'd been allowed through the wards, but the ghosts had made it clear he wasn't allowed back into the home without a fight. Even if he came in alone, my wards were still in place and would resist him.

I had no doubt, however, the biggest deterrent to him or any witch entering my home was the incredible power of the spirits who kept my home running.

I knew all that, yet I also knew it wouldn't be the last time Cary would be invited over. Owen needed friends—more than I did. I could sense that. Cary was definitely a friend in the making for Owen, and if I was being honest, I preferred a strong guardian to be with him when he wasn't with me.

The dark forces had their own rules they followed, and that usually meant that they wouldn't come after an innocent. I also knew not all dark forces followed the rules, and from what Owen had told me about seeing the dark not once but twice... That deserved being wary over.

I could sense that something that wasn't right. Maybe if I wasn't so new at this, I'd be able to figure it out, but as of yet, I couldn't quite tell what we needed to fear.

Luckily, Cary and the witches at his law firm would be a significant deterrent. I understood that most dark entities preferred to hate in the shadows, not in the sunshine. That didn't mean he was completely safe. He couldn't be with me and ever be completely safe.

I made a mental note to talk to Orville and the rest tomorrow. Maybe if they understood why it was important, they wouldn't be quite as upset. I almost snickered out loud at how preposterous that was. They hated the witches, and if my understanding was correct, they had every right to.

I rolled over, causing Owen to do the same. He spooned up against me, and I kissed the sweet softness of his neck. I fell asleep with images of us together like this for years to come, and suddenly, my heart was bursting with happiness.

Of all the ways to fall asleep, this had to be one of the best.

When I woke the following morning, Owen was already gone. I thought it strange that I hadn't noticed him leave. Since I'd begun getting these powers, I was keenly aware of where everyone was, even the ghosts.

I could estimate how many entities were within my walls, and I guessed there were around two hundred at the moment. The basement appeared to be a hub for them. I considered talking to the parchment about that but realized if the old wizard had tolerated it, I could trust that he knew what he was doing.

I got up and showered, then wandered down to the kitchen, where I heard Owen speaking to someone. When I felt the other's presence, I was surprised. I entered the kitchen, and a very young-looking male ghost stood kneading dough on the counter.

When he saw me, he began to fade, but I held my hand up. "You have no reason to fear me," I quickly said. "Please, stay, I can tell you and Owen were enjoying each other's company."

The ghost flickered in and out a few times, then solidified. Then he nodded to me without speaking. I went over and kissed Owen. "What smells so good?" I asked.

Owen looked at the ghost and winked. "Lucious, why don't you tell him? I'm going to run to the restroom, but I'll be right back. Oh, and before you leave, I want you to show me how you did the cinnamon rolls."

He disappeared around the corner, and I looked at our shy cook. "If my nose is correct, those rolls are almost done?" I asked, and the ghost smiled.

"Yes," he said smiling his face showing how shy he must be, "they are almost done."

I could tell something significant had just happened. Orville had made it clear that Cook, as they'd called him, didn't like to be seen. Now Lucious, clearly the cook they'd been referring to, was not only being seen but communicating with us.

"I could use one or a thousand about now," I said, and my stomach growled.

Lucious chuckled. "There are rolls cooling in the basket behind you," he said, and I turned and saw the basket sitting on the butler's pantry shelf covered with a towel.

"Can I have three?" I asked when I pulled the towel off, and the amazing scent hit me harder.

Lucious laughed. "You're the boss. You can have as many as you want. I'm making more now," he said.

I plopped three on a plate and sat across the island from where Lucious was still kneading. When I bit into the cinnamon roll, my mouth burst with flavor. "Oh my God, I might be in love. Lucious, can ghosts marry the living?" I asked just as Owen came in behind me.

"Get in line. I've already proposed," he said but bent over and kissed my neck before sitting beside me, stealing one of my rolls, and stuffing it in his mouth.

"Oh, Damian, do you want coffee? Lucious said they get the beans from...what's the name of the place?" he asked.

Lucious, who was blushing, which I didn't know ghosts could do, answered, "Soratories Beanery."

"Yeah, please," I said as I continued devouring the amazing rolls while Owen poured coffee and the ghost in front of us continued working.

When I tasted the coffee, I moaned with pleasure. "Lucious, this is amazing. The best coffee in Seattle, which is saying a lot. Where is this beanery?" I asked.

Lucious shrugged. "Not where you can get to it. Okay, maybe you can, but Owen can't," he said without looking up.

"Oh, a ghostly establishment?" I said, and Lucious snickered.

"Yes, something like that."

"I don't understand," Owen stated as he sat down. "How can ghosts make stuff that we can eat and drink? I mean, no offense, but I've never heard of all this happening anywhere else."

Images flowed through my mind with explanations of how things worked. I glanced over at Lucious, who made no attempt to explain, clearly leaving it to me.

"Essence," I told Owen. "Ghosts don't eat food or drink like we do. But all things have an essence. So, just like when they're alive, they can make food. They can also participate in our food rituals, correct?" I asked Lucious, who nodded.

"But that still doesn't explain how Lucious can cook for us, and have we even ever been shopping? Where do the ingredients come from?" he asked.

I laughed. "I think my predecessor is responsible. I can't see his actions, not like I can understand magic and the process of magical things, but Lucious, am I right to assume that the old wizard before me did something to make essence accessible to the living?"

"Yes, that's correct. Owen, I can show you how to make the rest of the rolls now if you wish."

Owen hopped up and went over to Lucious's side of the island. "We use butter here," he said, pointing at the bowl. "Smear it on really well."

I watched as Lucious had Owen do one step after another until the rolls were cut and put to one side to continue rising. "So, the wizard...opened up the possibility that ghosts can create in the realm of the living. Is that why so many ghosts reside here?" I asked.

Lucious didn't respond at first, but finally, he nodded. "You should ask Orville," he said, then sighed. "Are you going to kick us out or give us to the witches?" he suddenly asked, his ghostly face blooming red.

"Of course I'm not!" I replied, surprised at the question.

"You let a witch into your home, something the other wizard never did. Everyone is saying you aren't going to be the ally Elias was."

"Oh," I said and shook my head. "I...Lucious, I assure you, I will never allow the witches to come into my home and disrupt your lives. You have all been nothing but generous to us. Look at you. Even now, you've cooked us this amazing breakfast. Orville has been nothing less than helpful, as have Alice and Emma."

"Then why would you allow a witch into...into our safe space?" he asked.

I sighed, then shook my head. "First, because I didn't understand the significance of inviting him over until, well, until he came through the wards. Second, because Owen and Cary are friends. If Owen is to live here, he has the right to have friends, does he not?"

Lucious sighed. "I can't speak for the other residents of your home, but for me, having a witch here, knowing what they do to us, was like a slap in the face."

I waved my finger, solidifying Lucious's hand and putting mine on his. "I assure you, Lucious, I didn't mean to offend you or the others. I am appreciative of all you've done for us."

Lucious seemed shocked by the touch; then he became a bit emotional. He stared at our hands and sighed before pulling back, his physical hand returning to spirit form.

"You should talk to them, not just Orville, but all of them. This has been a safe haven for us for a long time. None of us want to give that up."

"Is that why you let us see you?" I asked, and slowly, Lucious nodded.

"I-I was like you two," he said. "Seattle was growing so fast. World War I was over, and buildings were going up everywhere. It was an exciting time. I started going down to Skid Row right after the war ended. I was young, but I knew I liked other men. There was nowhere else to go. I had a boyfriend a lot older than me. I'd just had my twentieth birthday, and he was in his late thirties, but he was wealthy. He owned a few hotels, including the one I worked at. One night, I'd just come out of the casino, one of the few places you could go back then to dance with other guys when I was attacked. I fell, my life slowly pouring out of me, and I saw my lover. Apparently, I had become a liability to him."

Lucious sighed and shook his head. "I died at the hands of the man I thought I loved. I wasn't ready to cross over. I wanted to understand what had happened. Why he'd chosen to kill me. I haunted him for the rest of his life and watched, unable to stop him as he did the same thing to three other young men. Finally, I figured out it wasn't me or the other guys he hated, it was himself, and because the world was unforgiving and hated us because of who we were, he got away with it. The old fart died of old age, never held accountable for what he did."

Lucious gazed up at me then. "The changes in the world didn't help me. Nothing did until the wizard opened his home to us. I was able to feel alive again, to come to terms with myself as a homosexual man. Now, you are here, and you are just like me or like I was. I've never allowed myself to be seen by the living, not until now, not even with the old wizard. I came here today and am here now with you, allowing you to see me because you represent hope, and I can't stand the thought of that going away."

Lucious paused, and I could tell he was imploring me to understand. Owen came around the island, and when he went in for the hug, I did the spell required for Lucious to become physical enough for Owen to make contact.

Tears fell from the ghost's eyes as Owen pulled him tight. "I'm so sorry, Lucious. Please understand we would never hurt you. Not intentionally."

As before, when Lucious pulled back, his body reverted to ghost form. "Okay, enough of that, Owen," he said, pointing toward the tray of rolls. "Those are ready to go into the oven."

Owen smiled and quickly did as he asked. "Lucious," I said. "I will speak with the others. Thanks for letting me know."

I kissed Owen's cheek, then walked over to the back room, where the stairs led down into the basement, the epicenter of the ghostly home. I felt the pressure build as I descended the steps. By the time I was at the bottom, I was surrounded. Orville stood before me, his face set.

"I've come to talk about yesterday," I said, and a mumble of frustration wafted around the room.

"I know you were upset, and for that, I apologize, but I don't apologize for inviting one of Owen's friends over. I spoke with Cook," I said, instinctively knowing that's how the ghosts referred to him. "He was afraid I was about to sever our relationship with you, and I will tell you now, nothing is further from the truth. I'm a new wizard. So new, I didn't understand the relationship between witches and ghosts. Had I understood, I would've approached the situation differently, but Owen...Owen lives here too, and he needs friends, relationships. My predecessor set much of this up. He put us in the hands of the witches to help keep us safe. I don't yet understand his reasoning, but I will," I said, looking at Orville, who had a better relationship with the old wizard.

He nodded. "You all see it's as I said, the young wizard is building alliances."

I was pleased to hear Orville had defended me. "I... I'm only beginning to glimpse the danger we are all in. The dark has been gathering. Elias told me it's been gathering since long before he departed. They are planning something, and none of us know what, not even him. Alliances are imperative, even with the witches. I disapprove of their ways. You should not be forced to cross over until you're ready." As images of nasty ghosts filled my mind, I quickly added, "I will only condone the forced removal of a ghost if they are actively disrupting the balance of light and dark or are hurting the living without cause. Like Elias, I will not judge unless I'm forced to."

I felt the wave of acceptance at my words. These were Elias's allies, more than any other. I was sure of that, even though I hadn't spoken to him yet. However, I most certainly would today.

"Okay, so are we forgiven?" I asked the room, although I was facing Orville.

I felt nods all around me, then sighed. "Okay, I'm going to get out of your hair, but from now on, please, let me know if you have concerns. You can go through Orville, or you know, set up a time to come sit with me. With the sheer number of you, I don't think I can handle you coming in and out without boundaries, but Orville, Emma, and Alice are all good resources. If you need to speak with me, and probably even Owen, just set up a time to do so."

Orville was smiling, so I figured I'd said the right thing. I waved and returned up the stairs, feeling like I had.

Lucious and Owen were still chatting in the kitchen, so I wandered up to the attic and pulled out the parchment. Time to have Elias fill me in on the ghosts of my home, even if it was a little late. Late was better than never.

Chapter Twenty-Eight

OWEN

Lucious and I had an immediate connection. I mean, he was only a little younger than me when he died, but now, considering he was over a century old, he was significantly older than me and had grown up the second generation of a pioneer family who'd settled in the Midwest, there was still symmetry in the coming out process. I'd grown up in Illinois, and he'd grown up around southern Iowa, but our eras were vastly different.

It was fun to compare notes though. At least now he'd stopped being afraid we were out to get him and his friends.

By the time I helped him get the dishes cleaned up, and he took the rolls away—I assumed to the mysterious others Orville had mentioned or maybe to the basement for the ghosts to enjoy—Damian was back in the attic. I could sense he needed time, so I went to my little bedroom to study and opened my laptop to get a head start on work for next week.

Shadow hadn't contacted me again, which was disappointing. Maybe when Molly came around again, I could ask her for details. I could use a boost with the firm, especially now I understood I was the only one there who wasn't a witch.

I didn't know if being a witch helped with the practice of law, but I had to assume it did. If most of the clients for our firm were magical, I'd need to bring in the nonmagical kind if I wanted to keep working there.

Once I got a lot of the work done that the partners, aka Cary, had given me for the week, I began exploring where to get more clients. Then I got the idea of putting out an ad. I'd speak with Cary about that on Monday. Maybe he could help me fashion it so the partners approved.

If the magical community had more people like me, nonmagical support, or even friends who needed regular law work, maybe that could be my in. I mean, I couldn't do magic, but I could help with contracts. It all hurt my head to think about. What was I doing? I didn't fit into this world or, at least, not well.

I lived here with Damian, a legacy wizard, who owned a house full of ghosts, who were all a bit pissy, and apparently, that was my fault since Damian had invited Cary for me. Then there's the firm I had moved to Seattle to work for, and they were a bunch of witches, meaning I wasn't needed.

God, what a strange mess. I ended up going to my bed and lying down. When I fell asleep, I dreamed of odd shapes flowing around me. It was almost as if they were trying to lure me out of the house and into the street.

I was woken by a sound outside my door. I quickly opened it to see Damian standing in front of me, his face full of concern. "Did they get to you?" he asked.

I shook my head. "Get to me? Who?" I asked at once, thinking of the ghosts.

"The dark forces?" I heard Orville say behind him, and Damian began studying me, not answering Orville. He sighed and pulled me into a hug.

"Orville, I just spoke to Elias," he said as he held me. "We need to reinforce the perimeter, but this time with essence. The dark has started their offensive, and," he said, pulling me back and assessing me again, "it appears they've decided to attack me through Owen."

१

CHAPTER TWENTY-NINE

DAMIAN

I WAS WORKING WITH Elias through the parchment, reviewing how his alliance with the ghosts had helped keep the balance between dark and light. When I told him about my encounter, he explained just how close to blowing up the alliance I'd come.

"Ignorance isn't bliss here," I'd told him.

"True, but I assure you, even though this felt dire, your effort to reconciliate likely endeared you to the residents. I feared the relationship with them could be in jeopardy once I passed."

We'd spent the morning reviewing the dos and don'ts of working with them, and he helped me distinguish between working with the ghosts and taking advantage of them. Wizards made alliances, sorcerers used them.

Apparently, sorcery was not good as it often involved using the ghost's essence against their will. Not cool, and doing it also damaged the sorcerer's soul. Nope, not interested in that.

We were just about done with our lesson when the back of my brain began to itch. I know that's a weird way to explain it, but it's exactly what it felt like. "Um, Elias, I-I think we're being invaded."

I closed my eyes and focused on the source of concern, explaining it to Elias. "Owen," we both said at the same time.

"Get to him now," Elias said, but I was already running toward the attic door.

I got to the first floor, where I could feel the invasion the strongest. Someone was trying to influence Owen. I immediately invoked my staff and severed the source of the attack, quickly adding wards to prevent it from happening again. When Owen opened the door to his bedroom, I could tell he'd been asleep.

I checked him over, and besides feeling elements of the dark magic still surrounding him, I could see he was confused and sleepy, but otherwise he looked to be okay. I got Orville to help me pull essence into the property's wards. I just had to thank all that was good I'd had a chance to make things better with the ghost, so he'd be willing to help.

"The witch," Orville said once I was done.

"Maybe," I replied because it was a bit suspicious that energy was allowed into the home that shouldn't have been able to come in through the wards. "I don't think so though, Orville. The witch, Cary, wasn't allowed in Owen's room. You all kept the boundaries around the rest of the room intact. In fact, I know you added your own," I said, chuckling.

Orville nodded but then looked at Owen. "I don't trust the witches for reasons you already know, but I agree, something else happened here. Someone got through Elias's wards, not to mention yours and ours. Young Owen, you should take this as a warning," he said, and I turned around to see a concerned expression on Owen's face.

"What...what happened? Did you see anything?" I asked.

Owen nodded. "Yes, sort of. It was in my dreams though. Something or someone was trying to get me to go outside."

"Wait," Orville said. "I know how we can tell for sure. I don't want it back in this house, but we've buried the talisman the witch gave us yesterday in the backyard. You should be able to use it to track whether his energy was used to invade us."

I nodded as images filled my mind of how to do that very thing. "Yes. Owen, I'll need you too," I said. Owen threw on shoes, not bothering to dress, and we followed Orville out the back door and into the garden. He pointed at a patch of disturbed ground, and I quickly dug up Cary's necklace.

It was covered in mud, so I apologized to Owen, but I wanted to do this before the energy that still encircled Owen dispersed. "Sorry," I said as I put the necklace over his head, mud and all.

Nothing happened except that Cary's necklace seemed to absorb the rest of the energy surrounding Owen. A sure sign that Cary's magic was from the light, and whatever attacked Owen had been dark.

"Was it Cary?" Owen asked.

I shook my head. "No, but I think you could use one of these if Cary is of a mind to make another one for you," I said.

Owen nodded, his eyes still wide with concern. "Okay, Orville," I called, and the ghost appeared beside me. "I'm going to take this up to the attic. I need to analyze it to see if the positive energy of Cary's magic can help me figure out where the dark energy it absorbed came from."

Orville looked at the necklace with disgust but made way for us to walk past him and into the house. I normally wouldn't involve Orville or anyone with the ways of wizardry, but since yesterday, I sorta felt like I needed to.

I didn't remove the muddy necklace from Owen until we got there and sat down. Then, I asked Owen to remove it and place it next to the parchment. "I dare not touch it, as I think my powers would immediately destroy the darkness, and I want Elias's help figuring out its source."

Owen just nodded and did as I asked. I picked up the quill and activated the parchment. "Is Owen okay?" Elias asked.

"Yes, Elias, I'm fine," Owen responded.

"I have a necklace that's absorbed the energy that attacked Owen. Can you help us distinguish where the attack came from?" I asked.

For the rest of the afternoon, with Elias's limited help, we tried to trace the darkness. Since he could only communicate through the parchment, it didn't work. However, Elias confirmed there was no way the energy could've reached Owen in his room if a witch, or at least a similar power, hadn't been there.

That meant it wasn't Cary. The only other person I could think of was Molly. But she wasn't a magical being. She wasn't even what we would classify as a source of light, like Owen. So, how would her being here give the darkness power to come through the wards?

It couldn't, plain and simple. Molly couldn't send power to impact Owen, nor could she be manipulated to do so. That just wasn't how magic worked.

That meant something else was at play, but nothing I could think of would have the power to break through my wards unless an army of darkness came at me all at once. I was powerful enough to hold the darkness back, and I doubted my or Elias's wards would ever be impacted without that full-on assault.

Chapter Thirty

OWEN

I WASN'T TOO KEEN on leaving the safety of the house, even after Cary agreed to meet me Monday morning with a necklace like the one he'd worn to our house on Friday.

"You okay?" Cary asked after I donned the necklace and strapped the seat belt on.

"Um, no, not really. What could've infiltrated the wards?" I asked.

Cary shrugged. "I don't know, but if I'm going to guess, it's someone you let in the door."

"Molly?" I asked, and Cary shrugged. "Not on her own. She doesn't have the power. She's not a witch, and as far as I could tell, she was only human. However, we are watching."

"Wait, you're watching Molly? No one will hurt her?" I asked, and Cary immediately shook his head.

"No, of course not. Witches have a bad reputation, some of which is earned, but we don't interfere with humans' and nonmagical people's lives. Let's just say that's a lesson we learned the hard way."

I cringed, remembering the witch trials. "Okay, so, am I safe? Damian thinks I am with you and my bosses, you all being witches and stuff."

Cary laughed. "You're safe as can be with us, but to be honest, I am surprised even a dark entity would dare take on a wizard. It's a good way to find yourself six feet under."

I paused, thinking about that. "Damian isn't violent."

"Really? If someone tried to hurt you or Molly? You don't think he'd react?"

I shook my head. "I don't know, Cary. I... It's weird to think about."

Cary took a deep breath and let it out slowly. "For now, don't think about it. Let's go have a carby breakfast and copious amounts of coffee, and then we'll go sleep it off in the office."

I laughed. "You know your bosses are witches right?"

Cary just laughed. "You're learning. Okay, no sleeping it off, but I did let them know you were attacked this weekend. They're on high alert, and it was even Mr. Harrison's suggestion that we take the morning to settle you back in."

I laughed, thinking about my boss and more about Cary. "You mean to pry information from me. Cary, you might be a witch, but you're still a total gossip queen. You think I missed that?"

Cary eyed me and put the car in drive. "Lucky for you, you're the boyfriend of a powerful wizard, or I might be tempted to turn you into a frog or something for such a comment."

I batted the hand he had placed on the gear shift and laughed. "You're a light witch, and you can't turn people into frogs for telling the truth."

Cary laughed out loud, and honestly, it was probably because I didn't know what the hell I was talking about, but at least he was amused by me.

Chapter Thirty-One

DAMIAN

"Molly, for real, call me back. Are you mad at me or something?" I hung up, frustrated. Molly would sometimes get pissed about something or another, but she never totally ghosted me. Of course, she'd been working hard, so I was probably just overthinking.

I was so exhausted with all the training I was doing. Elias might be on the other side of the veil, but that didn't mean the man wasn't working me to death. Of course, most of the time, my powers were intuitive, and that was helpful, but I still screwed things up, like I had with inviting Cary over and pissing off my ghostly companions.

We were practicing discernment, as Elias called it. "You need to be able to recognize the energy around you." I'd already visited a place known to be frequented by the dark, so I could feel what it was like to be around them.

Elias had also given me directions to a part of my neighborhood where a horrible murder had taken place, where the energy was still maleficent. He'd also sent me to find the light energies, places where I could recharge if I needed to.

"Not all entities of the dark or light know who they are. Like your Owen. He is a light energy, but he's only aware of that because you and his employers told him so."

That made sense. When I figured out how to discern energy, I began calling Molly, hoping to figure out what powers or energies were surrounding her. My memories told me she was neutral. Humans with no power, and most animals, tended to be. The exception being cats, of course, as you would expect, they were seldom neutral. Foxes were another animal that, according to Elias, tended to be either light or dark energies.

I didn't want to think Molly was behind the attack on Owen. Everything in me told me she hadn't been, at least not intentionally, but she'd been in the home several times now and had access to Owen's living space.

Although that wasn't technically true either, unless Owen had told her, she'd never been in his little hidey-hole behind the shelves in the library. Who had? No one, not even the group who'd come with Molly that first time for the seance had gone to the room behind the shelves. Yet someone had to have gotten in.

Elias had assured me he never allowed entities into his home. The ghosts were the only spiritual beings who'd ever come in. They were not friends of the dark, nor of any witches or power wielders, so that wasn't the problem. No, it'd only been since

I'd been in the position of wizard that someone had breached the wards.

Elias had instructed me how to rebuild the wards, and mixed with my intuition, I knew nothing would be coming for Owen again. I wouldn't allow another entity into the home again until I understood who and what they were.

Those were the consequences of being new at something and not knowing what I was doing. Of course, Elias had repeatedly told me that when he'd started, he'd made many more mistakes, even with the wisdom of the scroll and his predecessor to help.

Apparently, the scroll was all the help he'd had. He'd had to live on the streets during America's Great Depression, barely scraping by. No money, no direction, no place to live. All while he fought the powers who wished to disrupt the balance between darkness and light.

"Of course, you should know that you will need allies in the darkness as well," Elias told me during one of our training sessions. "Don't become conceited enough to think that all dark wants to do is disrupt the balance of light and dark. Most wish to maintain what we have. It's only the rare few that would actively disrupt the flow."

Of course, that conversation had confused me. It's easy to think in absolutes, although intuitively, I knew what he was saying was true. Science had taught us all that darkness ruled the universe. It was only in small pockets where it didn't reign supreme. In the whole scheme of things, the sun, in all its glory, was also just temporary. Eventually, darkness would reclaim even this tiny speck of light.

I didn't know how black holes came into play, just that they did. The ultimate darkness was at the center of all things light. It didn't make sense that dark would care since, ultimately and quite naturally, it would always reclaim space.

I shook off my philosophical thoughts. Elias was no help with those questions and confirmed he'd had the same ones when he'd been alive.

With my instructions in hand, I walked around the city, identifying energies as I went. Most were benign. Some surprisingly bright, some definitely dark. Thanks to Elias's advice, I began to distinguish between those dark energies which were fine, such as a bar located just the other side of Pike's Place. I even went in, ordered a drink and sat there, assessing the atmosphere. Nothing was dangerous despite the very dark elements of the place.

I was just about to leave when a man caught my eye. We assessed each other briefly before he smiled and bowed his head toward me. My intuition indicated he was a changeling of some sort, not of this world, but not a danger either. My intuition also told me one day I might need to rely on this creature for help.

I found a similar place, a florist this time, with high light energy. I walked in and was immediately uncomfortable. Arrogance and superiority flowed around me. The proprietor, a man who appeared to be in his late sixties seemed to be pushing people away. I left without spending any money.

Okay, so I was beginning to get it. The dark wasn't always bad, and the light was certainly not always good. That probably went doubly true for the witches. I stepped inside Owen's place of business and was immediately accosted by the energies that flowed there.

Not all were light. "Witches are a diverse mix of the light and dark," Elias had instructed me when I'd asked whether Cary might be up to no good. "However, when they use dark energy, or dark magic as some call it, you can sense it immediately."

I lingered outside the door before going in. Although I knew the witches could detect my presence, I wanted to gather and discern the energy for myself. No one with the intuition I had would call the energy here benign. Neither the bar nor the florist was as intense as this was.

However, there were no indications that the powers that flowed here were any threat to me, Owen, or the balance I'd been entrusted to keep. I stepped into the office and was met by Cary, the two partners of the firm, and even an older female witch I hadn't met before.

"Mr. Richards, to what do we owe the honor?" Mr. Stages asked.

"I'm just getting to know my community, but thought I'd stop by to see if Owen would like to go with me to lunch."

Owen came around the corner then, and after looking at his bosses and the others, he turned a concerned expression toward me.

"Oh, well, that makes sense. Owen, are you free for lunch?" the older partner asked.

Owen shrugged. "I... maybe?" he asked more than said.

I chuckled. "Everyone can stand down. I was just testing my abilities to discern energy. I'm sorry if I caused any upset."

All four witches scrutinized me, but it was Cary who shifted the tension. "As always, Damian, we are grateful for your patronage. Owen, why don't you go on and have lunch now? I'll take mine when you return."

Owen nodded, then rushed back to his office to get his jacket. I followed him outside and couldn't help but laugh once we were out of earshot, and I was pretty sure it was out of range for the witches to magically detect me.

"What was that about?" Owen asked.

"My homework from Elias seems to have caused a little upset with your employer."

Owen looked at me funny, then asked, "The discernment thing you mentioned?"

I nodded. "Yes, Elias said I need to discern the spirit. Not all dark is bad. Not all light is good. He put me on the path to figuring out which is which. I'm sure it was a bit of a setup, though. Luckily, the witches you work for are friendly. Otherwise, I think my snooping around would've been seen as a challenge."

"So, Elias is setting you up?" he asked concerned.

"Yeah, I mean, learning not to piss off the magical beings around me is a big part of being a wizard. I don't think it's possible to avoid it entirely though. Sometimes, as a wizard, I think my job will be to challenge the different powers that be. My intuition tells me that as well."

Owen shook his head. "Where are we going?" he asked, and at first I didn't know what he meant. When I turned to him with a confused expression, he chuckled. "You said you'd come to meet me for lunch. Where are we going to have lunch?"

"Oh, yeah, um, I want to go check on Molly. Hopefully, she's at her favorite hang-out. It's on the other side of the neighborhood though. Do you think you have time to go all the way over there?"

Owen thought for a moment, then smiled. "Yeah, I have a potential client...Shadow. I think that's her name?" he asked, and I nodded.

"It's hard to forget Shadow, and trust me, I've known her a lot longer than you. Why?"

"She told me the day we met that she wanted to hire me, remember?"

I nodded. He'd told me that after we left the bar. She did well financially in her musical performances, and he'd do well to sign up as her attorney.

"Okay, well, let's go," I said, and Owen nodded, then took out his phone. I could tell he was texting Cary, telling him he'd be late getting back.

I doubted they'd mind unless something was going on at work I wasn't aware of. Which it could've been. Owen didn't discuss his work with me that much.

I hoped that changed soon though. I had tried hard not to leave Owen out of my experiences as a wizard, and I wanted to know about his life too. Yes, they were vastly different, but that didn't mean I wanted my world to overshadow his.

We walked hand in hand all the way across the neighborhood to the little bar Molly and her friends had adopted long before I started coming along. The place was small and tucked in the back corner of an alley behind one of the neighborhood commercial pockets the area was known for.

I'd never felt uncomfortable there before, never felt anything really, but the moment I saw the bar, chills rolled down my spine. I hadn't been there since the day I met Owen. That had been before I'd begun to hone my wizard powers.

I paused before going in. The atmosphere was anything but welcoming now that I felt it through my magic. I took a deep breath, knowing my friends were in there, and followed Owen through the front door.

Shadows played along the walls, and not all were there because of where the light cast them. There were also magical creatures lurking in the corners. I recognized some of them, but none had felt particularly dangerous before. Now, they eyed me warily as I walked toward where my friends and I always hung out.

Molly wasn't there. In fact, the only ones in our group that were there were two of the guys I'd dated in the past and a couple I didn't recognize. Luckily, none of them seemed to be dark, although as I stared at my exes, I realized I'd missed the glimpses of darkness that skirted around them. They were the opposite of Owen. They were like dark torches. "Have any of you seen Molly lately?" I asked.

They all shook their heads, and then Owen asked about Shadow, getting the same response.

"If you see Molly, please tell her I'm looking for her," I said, and the four of them nodded but didn't respond. Not that I expected them to. My exes might not totally hate me, but they weren't fond of me either.

"Don't you want to get a drink or something to eat?" Owen said as I began pulling him out the front door.

I shook my head. "No, not here," I said, not even trying to hide my thoughts or opinions. I might have just seen the place for what it was, but I couldn't help but guess the threatening characters that lined the walls certainly knew who and what I was—probably had for a while.

Once outside the bar, I took a deep cleansing breath and immediately recognized spells stuck to me and Owen. "Well, shit," I said as I let my intuition show me how to break them.

"What?" Owen asked.

"Nothing. Come on, I need to find spring water," I said, leading him away from the bar to an old artesian fountain a few blocks away. I'd known about the place for a while. It used to be used as a water fountain, but I doubted anyone wanted to use it for that these days. I stuck my hand under the water and then wiped up and down my entire body, then did the same with Owen.

He didn't say anything, even when I grabbed his crotch, hoping to lighten the mood. "What?" I asked when I finished removing all the negative spells that clung to us.

"What happened back there?" he asked.

"That's not a good place, but I didn't know that until now. We won't be going back in there anytime soon, because... Let's just say we aren't welcome."

"Me either?" he asked, and I nodded.

"Yeah, sorry, Owen, but you were with me, and the magical entities there would know we are together. You should avoid going in there. In fact, I'm going to discourage Molly from going too."

Owen chuckled. "I have a feeling you aren't going to have much luck telling your girlfriend what she can and can't do."

That caused me to laugh out loud. "Oh, well, yeah, you've got her number. Okay, I'll treat you to lunch at my next favorite hangout; then you should take a taxi back to work. Do you have the necklace Cary made you?" I asked, and Owen nodded, pulling it out so I could see.

"Good, keep that on. I definitely feel something is going on. I'm not sure what, but it seems to have its roots in the bar we just came from. I'm afraid I walked right into it. Literally.

Again, my ignorance seems to have caused me to fuck up. Regardless, I'd rather you be safe than sorry."

"What are your plans? Are you worried about Molly?" Owen asked, and I nodded.

"Sort of, I mean, we've been coming to this bar for ages. I doubt they'll harm her, but I'll feel better when I check on her."

Owen leaned over and kissed me. "Go on, I'll get that taxi now. I can grab something close to the office, and you can relieve your mind about Molly."

I smiled. He was such a considerate guy. I kissed him and waited until his taxi showed, hanging out at the park where the fountain was. Once he was gone, I headed toward Molly's work. I'd start there, and if she wasn't at work, I'd walk over to her apartment, which wasn't far.

If something had happened, I'd know soon enough.

CHAPTER THIRTY-TWO

OWEN

I HAD TEXTED CARY, telling him I'd be late, mostly because I had wanted to reconnect with Damian and Molly's friend Shadow. He already knew I was pursuing her as a client, and truth be known, I was just doing paperwork at the office at this point.

If I didn't round up some clients, I'd be relegated to that from now on. He sent back a thumbs-up, which was a good indication of how much Damian had freaked them out. Cary, even though we were becoming friends, still gave me a lot of shit about being gone from the office, even when I had every reason and excuse.

It was almost like he was one of the partners. Come to think of it, in more ways than not, he was. I might not be a powerful witch or wizard, but I knew my bosses trusted Cary to run the practice.

I rehashed in my mind what had happened. When Damian and I had stepped into the bar, I immediately knew something wasn't right. I might not have magic, but I did have good instincts about people and places. Damian stiffened before we even got inside. He was looking around the bar, and after asking about Molly, he wasted no time getting us out.

The whole spell thing was strange. He led me to a small park not far away and used the well water to wipe away the negativity. I had actually felt the change. I probably wouldn't have known it had he not told me what was happening, but once we left the bar, I felt heavy. Like I'd put on a heavy jacket or something.

Once he finished with the water spell thing, it was like the jacket had been removed. Subtle, but definitely detectable.

He was worried about Molly. I could tell that, and although he offered to treat me to lunch, I wanted him to check on her as well. I had a feeling something wasn't right. Maybe that was my own source of intuition, but it was as if the universe was telling me to let him go.

The taxi took me back to my office, and I sidestepped the front door to go to my favorite little restaurant to order a salad. I didn't get a hundred feet before someone blocked my path. I glanced up to say excuse me when I recognized the man from a few weeks ago who'd left bruises on my arms.

He grabbed me before I could step away, but this time, he pulled his hands back the moment they touched me. His face seemed to waver, and I glimpsed what appeared to be a snake's face instead of human. "Witch," I heard him say, although his mouth didn't move.

I was just about to argue that I wasn't a witch when I heard footsteps behind me. "Owen, are you okay?" Cary asked.

I turned to nod, but when I glanced back, the weird man was gone. "What the hell just happened?" I asked, surprised by his sudden disappearance.

"Nothing good, that's for sure," Mr. Stages said. "Owen, we need you to come back to the office now. Cary, run ahead and ask Mrs. Patterson to prepare the scrying spell. We need to figure out what just attacked Owen."

Cary nodded and ran back to the office. Mr. Harrison and Mr. Stages both checked me over then. They examined my arms where the man or snake thing, whatever he was, had tried to grab me and looked at one another strangely.

"Have you seen the man before?" Mr. Harrison asked.

I nodded. "Yeah, a few weeks ago, why?"

"Did he touch you?" Mr. Stages asked, and I nodded.

"Show me," he said and I undid my shirt sleeve and pushed it up to show him where the bruise still showed.

"Because it appears that he marked you when he did," Mr. Stages said. "I'm guessing had you not been wearing Cary's amulet, he'd have done much worse this time."

I reached up and touched the necklace. "He jerked back when he touched me. Was that because of this?" I asked, pulling the necklace out of my shirt.

"Likely, but we need to remove the marks from your arm. Then you should have your wizard create his own security around you."

"Wait, he marked me. Is that why I had the nightmare?" I asked.

The partners turned to one another and, without saying another word, began pulling me toward the office.

Once I was securely back in the building, Mr. Harrison picked my phone up and called someone. I heard Damian's voice on the other end of the line and Mr. Harrison telling him he should return to their office.

"Is Owen okay?" I heard him ask.

"He will be, but you need to come soon."

He hung up without saying goodbye, then Mrs. Patterson came in with a bowl of water. "Now, you sit still. I need to see what's going on," she said, placing the bowl on my desk after Mr. Harrison neatly stacked all the paperwork and laid it on the floor beside the file cabinet.

I watched, mesmerized, as she began to hum. The water rippled, and the partners, Mrs. Patterson, and I stared into it.

I didn't see anything, but Mrs. Patterson gasped and put her hand to her mouth. "Could it be? After all this time?"

The partners didn't respond, just watched whatever images they were seeing in the water. Then Mr. Stages reached into his pocket and pulled out an ancient-looking whiskey flask. He opened the lid and poured a greenish liquid into the water. It sizzled for several seconds before the water went placid again.

"Mrs. Patterson, take this outside and dump it into the sewer drain. I'll send Cary to remove any other residue once you're done."

The legal assistant nodded and disappeared to do as she'd been told. "Son," Mr. Harrison said. "You are in a great deal of trouble, and it's a total mess that none of us saw it. Your boyfriend is a new wizard, or he probably would've sniffed it out earlier. However, if we don't do something about it soon, I'm afraid there will be some serious consequences. Serious indeed."

Chapter Thirty-Three

DAMIAN

M Y NERVES WERE ALREADY on edge when I got to Molly's job, and they said they hadn't seen her in a couple of days.

"Did she call in sick?" I asked, and the woman shook her head but didn't respond verbally. It wasn't like her.

I left and walked toward her apartment just as I got a call from Mr. Harrison telling me I needed to come to Owen's office.

"Is Owen okay?" I asked, and they assured me he was but that I needed to come soon.

Molly first, I thought. If Owen was with the witches, I knew he was safe, and Molly, it was totally out of character for her not to return my phone calls, much less not call into work to let them know she wasn't coming in.

When I got to her apartment, I felt the darkness immediately. It felt inky, like someone had used a brush to wipe it on. I magically surrounded myself with safety wards, almost on autopilot, and knocked on the door.

There was no answer, but I knew there wouldn't be. Molly wasn't there. I knew she wasn't. I pulled my key out, the one I had to her home, and opened the door. I could smell it: swamp water, deep, dirty, and stagnant.

I slipped inside and felt the web of spells surrounding the room. It didn't take much to disarm them. Whoever put them there wasn't trying to do anything, probably because they knew I'd come searching for her.

It would take a lot more work to cleanse the place, but that was a concern for later. I searched for any clues as to where she was. I closed my eyes, pulling power to myself. When my staff automatically appeared in my hand, I knew there was a threat.

"Where is she?" I demanded, and I heard a chuckle. Nasty, antagonistic.

"Give him to us, and we'll trade."

"Give who to you? No, never mind. I will give you one warning and only one— You will return the innocent, or I will destroy you and everything around you."

The laughter grew. "Innocent indeed. I have taken only what has called to me. Bring me the man, bring him to me, and I will let your little darklings live."

I felt the presence disappear, and my heart fell. Darklings? I might not know all the ins and outs of being a wizard, but I did know if someone had played with the dark, I couldn't use light to rescue them. The fact he called Molly a darkling was bad. Really bad.

God, I hoped she hadn't done anything that would keep me from helping her. Who else was with her? I had no idea. The entity had said darklings, so I had to assume more than one soul was at stake.

There wasn't much more I could do, so I closed her door and locked it against the nonmagical world. I couldn't stop the magical ones from coming in and harming her, or hadn't before it was too late, but I could at least keep the thieves at bay.

I quickly cast a spell over the door to do just that and rushed out of the building, requesting a taxi as I went. When my buddy from my days driving pulled up, he laughed at me. "Did you lose your car?" he asked as I climbed in.

"Hey, Ed, I was just over on this side of town. I need to get to my boyfriend's office quickly. Can you go down Third Street?"

Ed gave me a side-eye but nodded. "Sure, no problem," he said and started off. I quickly group texted all our friends, asking everyone to check in and tell me if they'd seen Molly and informing them she hadn't shown up at work for the past two days.

Everyone except Shadow texted back. Well, at least now I knew who was with her, and Shadow was very likely a darkling. The woman was obsessed with the dark arts, as she called them.

She had no power. Even though I wasn't with her, I knew from memory at most she was a torch. She was no witch, no matter how much she wanted to be one. It was very likely that she was a dark source, though, similar to how Owen was a light source.

When I got to the office, I thanked Ed and gave him a hefty tip before rushing inside. "Damian," Cary said, concern all over his face. "I'm glad you're here. We need to begin the ritual now."

CHAPTER THIRTY-FOUR

OWEN

I HAD NO IDEA what was going on. The four witches I worked with each took a corner of the conference room, forcing me to remove my shirt so they could see the places where I'd been tagged and placed me in the middle of the room. "Hold still, we're going to begin the cleansing process," Mr. Harrison said.

They chanted, traded places, then chanted and did it again four times. Then Mr. Stages came over, checked my arms, and shook his head. "It didn't work."

"We need to wait for the wizard," Mr. Harrison said, and the other three nodded.

Mrs. Patterson got me a bottle of water and told me to stay put. "We want to get to work the minute your wizard friend gets here," she said. I made myself comfortable playing *Candy Crush* on my phone.

Half an hour later, Damian burst into the office. I saw him through the plate glass windows, and he looked concerned. He was pulled into the conference room by the others.

"What's this?" he asked when Mr. Stages had pointed toward my arms before going to his spot. "What the hell? Owen, when did this happen?" he asked.

"I...um, like the day we met, I think. That's when the weird man grabbed me. Remember I had bruises?"

Damian shook his head. "No, I don't remember bruises, but you did tell me some strange man manhandled you."

Damian leaned back, closing his eyes as if to think. "I need cayenne, and does anyone have mugwort?" he asked.

Mrs. Patterson nodded and dashed out of the room, then returned a few moments later with two small spice bottles. "Okay, you've begun the process to remove this with witch magic. I'm going to build upon your spells. That's the quickest and easiest way to remedy this. Um, Cary, do you have... I-I sense a small container, metal? Tin? I need that," Damian said, and Cary nodded and ran to his desk. I watched through the window as he pulled a small cookie tin out and dumped the contents into the trash before rushing back to the room.

"I guess I owe you some cookies," I said, but Cary didn't acknowledge my silliness. *Strange.*

Damian took it from him without acknowledgment and lifted me so I stood, then pulled my arms together until my elbows touched. He placed the cookie tin under my elbows and looked at the witches. "You should chant now," he said, and all four began the same strange chant they'd done before Damian had arrived.

Damian poured the contents of the two bottles into his hand, then waved his other hand over it until it turned into some strange liquid. My instincts told me it would be superhot to the touch, although I had no idea why.

The witches changed corners again. All the while, Damian stirred the contents in his hand. When the witches got to the fourth corner, Damian lifted his hand, and the contents turned to steam. His staff appeared in his hand, the hand that had held the contents just seconds before, and he pointed the staff at my arms, which were beginning to get achy from holding such an awkward position.

The steam began to swirl around my head, then moved down until it reached my arms.

I felt a searing pain in both upper arms and realized it was where the man had grasped me and where he'd tried to grasp me again today. I yelled out as the pain increased.

"What the fuck!" I yelled as the pain ran down my upper arms into my elbows. Then, a thick black tarlike substance poured out of my elbows and into the tin.

Fatigue washed over me. I swayed and fell back into the chair. Damian grabbed the lid of the cookie tin and slammed it on.

Then, with his staff, he touched the top of the tin, and it began to glow. The paint on the outside of the tin burned off immediately, and I caught a whiff of it as it dispersed. Then, I watched the tin transform into a smaller, denser box.

Finally, only a tiny, glowing orange cube remained. Damian touched his staff to it. The little cube attached itself to the top of his staff, and the whole thing disappeared back into Damian's hand.

When it was done, he shook his head. "I think we've got some serious problems. I hope you're ready for a fight."

Chapter Thirty-Five

DAMIAN

I HAD NOT BEEN prepared for the world I'd stepped into. I should've recognized that Owen had been tagged. The fact that it took the witches to find it, even after he and I had slept together repeatedly, told me how out of my depth I was.

The ritual, however, was easy enough. It required that I drain the poison out of his arms. Unfortunately, it'd grown, so I knew there would be more pain to remove it now than if we'd caught the tag early.

The four witches in Owen's law firm had already begun the process of removing the poison, so I decided it was easier to use their spell and finish it with my own than it was to take him back to the attic and use my powers on him. I intuitively knew the witches' way would hurt less and could be done quicker than my method.

I had a vast knowledge of the witches' magic. One of my predecessors had been a witch. That's what it felt like, at least. The knowledge must've come down from her.

Mugwort was needed to relax the muscles, and cayenne to force the blood to flow through the spell and drain the nastiness out of him and into the tin.

Luckily, tin was one of the metals that could be manipulated to hold magic, at least temporarily, and I sensed Cary had a tin container in his desk.

Once the spell was over, I collapsed on one of the chairs beside Owen, the four witches doing the same. "That was intense, and I'm afraid a glimpse of what's to come," I said.

"What do you see, wizard?" Mr. Harrison asked.

"There's a group of vipers gathering on the edge of town. They're angry. That's what I sense."

Mr. Stage's forehead creased, and I looked around the room to see the other three witches were equally concerned. "The vipers," Mr. Stages said. "They are a modern-day gang of thugs. Most aren't magical. All are somehow associated with the darkness. I...well, none of us thought they were a real threat to the overall balance of power."

"Apparently, they are or want to be. My friend Molly has been taken, and I assume so has our mutual friend Shadow, although I'm not certain. I went to Molly's place and was confronted by a disembodied entity. He told me to trade the man for her, although I don't know what man he meant."

I could tell they were all as confounded as I was. I'd taken Owen's hand and slowly sent him healing energy. He appeared very relaxed and maybe just a bit high from the act. But I figured that was fine, especially considering what we'd just put his poor body through.

"We need to figure out what man he meant," Mrs. Paterson said.

Owen replied. "I-I sorta think it's me."

We all turned toward him and stared for a few moments. I let go of his hand, afraid maybe I'd sent too much energy into him.

"I... I was the one who was attacked, and that guy tried to attack me again. They also came to me in my dream. They wanted me to come outside and kept enticing me. Cary even had to drive one of them off when they impersonated a taxi driver. If they're looking for a man to trade for Molly and Shadow, doesn't it make sense it would be me?"

The tag put on him certainly explained how they got past my wards. That mystery was solved, at least. What didn't make sense was why they wanted Owen. "I'm sorry, Owen," Cary said, saying the same thoughts I'd just had. "Why would they want you?"

He shrugged. "To screw with Damian? You all? I don't know. It seems like a good way to create havoc."

Cary chuckled. "Sorry, Owen, the powers that be never pay attention to nonmagicals. Not even those who are light or dark sources. No offense, but you don't even register on the chessboard as a pawn."

"Cary," Mrs. Patterson chastised, but Owen just laughed.

"I get it, and I'd agree, but I was the one attacked and tagged, as you called it. The man wanted me. He was trying to get to me and would've, had it not been for your necklace. Why would they want me otherwise?"

"Bait," I said before I could catch myself. "I'm so sorry, Owen, but I have to agree with you on that. They want you because of me, and just like Molly, they'd use you to get to me, to all of us."

I sighed at the reality of that. "Maybe you should consider staying somewhere else for a while. I-I don't want you to get hurt because of me. Maybe, you would be safe if they think we broke up."

"Psst," Mr. Harrison said. "They know you care about him. Even if you were to break up, he'd still be vulnerable because they know you'd come for him. No, Owen needs to stay put, and now the tag has been drained from him, they won't be able to cross your boundaries."

"I daresay," Mr. Stages added, "you shouldn't be inviting any other magical beings into your home though. We all appreciate the openness with us, especially Cary, but your home needs to be your refuge and a place for you to keep Owen safe."

Owen looked around the room and then at me. "Damian, you want to break up with me? I-I can stay somewhere else, with maybe a witch or someone that can watch out for me."

My eyes grew large at what Owen must've interpreted from my words. "No, no, Owen, I don't want you to go. I... It's just so dangerous. I don't want you to be in jeopardy because of whatever this is I've become."

He stared at me for several moments, then sighed. "I need some time to figure all this out, and I've got some more work to get done in my office...but we can talk tonight," he said, standing to go. I almost thought he'd sway, considering how much energy we'd taken from him to do the spell, but he remained strong. Maybe the energy flow I'd given him had been enough after all.

When he was gone, the four witches stared at me, none of us talking. "I don't want him to move out; it's just I don't want to put him at risk," I said more to myself than to them.

"Young wizard, your predecessor went to great lengths to create an environment where your perfect mate would be available for you. He often spoke of being lonely in the last decades of his life. He didn't want that for you. I'm not sure how he managed it, or why he was able to attract Owen to come work at our firm, but I believe you have an opportunity that none of your predecessors had. You should be very careful before squandering that."

I nodded, then stood to go. "I will need your help—not just yours, but the magical community you trust. I have resources you don't, and I will send out scouts to try to help me find Molly and anyone else being held with her. When they're found, I will need to take the vipers on. I know as a wizard, I should be able to do this alone, and I suspect I can, but being new and still developing a sense of the community, I'd prefer to have help so I don't mess things up or inadvertently get my friends killed."

Mr. Stages came over and placed his hand on the table in front of me. When he turned it over, palm up, in it was a small gemstone. "You have us and our coven. As the leader, I assure you we will come when you call."

I took the stone, and it was immediately absorbed into my skin. This was a huge honor, one that witches didn't bestow easily. I suspected they cared as much about Owen as they did for me. Cary had even liked Molly, although I didn't think it was enough for such a generous offer. If Molly and Shadow were indeed darklings, I'd need the witches more than ever. I wouldn't be able to protect them. Wizard's magic wouldn't allow it. However, the witches were freer, and their power was more forgiving when it came to the dark.

I nodded, left the conference room, then looked down the hall to where I knew Owen was. I was about to go that way to say goodbye when Cary came up behind me and put his hand on my arm. "Give him a moment," he said.

I decided not to wait because Cary was right, he needed space, and it was probably best if I just left.

Besides, I needed to get the ghosts started searching for Molly and whoever else was being held anyway. Then, I needed to figure out how to protect Owen. Of course, I also needed to ensure he understood I was there for him and I didn't want him to leave.

Shit, I'd screwed up. He thought I didn't want him. He couldn't be more wrong. I sighed heavily as I walked outside. I looked both ways, trying to discern if anything was amiss. Nothing seemed out of the ordinary, except now that I'd detected the vipers, I could feel them, like a small splinter or something. Annoying but not life-threatening.

I certainly hoped that applied to Molly. However it worked out, I needed to concentrate on her right now because I wasn't at all sure she wasn't in jeopardy. In fact, the more I thought about it, the more I believed she was.

Chapter Thirty-Six

OWEN

M Y HEART BROKE WHEN Damian said we should break
up. I guess I figured it was just a matter of time. I
opened my laptop and found a flight back to Illinois. The
so-called vipers were here in Seattle, and I was sure I'd be safe
there.

I wouldn't stay in someone's home if I wasn't wanted. That
was a simple fact. I gazed around the office and sighed. *This
is a ruse too.* I was here because Damian's predecessor had
been playing matchmaker, not because the law firm needed or
wanted a nonmagical attorney on their staff.

Hell, I hadn't had one damned client assigned to me since
I'd been here. Okay, I was a new graduate, and even in a regular
law firm, I probably wouldn't have had clients yet. Regardless,
I'd been given piles and piles of work better assigned to a legal
assistant than a licensed attorney.

I pulled my phone out and texted my mother.

> Me: Hey, Mom, I might need to come home for a bit, is that okay with you?

> Her: Yeah, what's wrong?

> Me: Boy troubles, nothing major.

> Her: Yes, I'm leaving for a legal conference in St. Louis, but you can dog sit for me while you're home. How long will you be here?

Honestly, I didn't know the answer to that. Just that I needed to go. It was all way too much, and I needed to get the hell out of this town.

I opened a document, typed a resignation letter, and printed it out. "Cary," I said via my phone, "can you come into my office for a moment?"

When he arrived, I handed him the letter. "So, I need to ask your advice, and I need you not to go running to Damian. Deal?"

Cary regarded me for a long time before he said, "I won't promise anything of the sort. You are not safe, and I can tell this letter isn't something you should be writing."

I took a deep breath and held it briefly before exhaling slowly. "Let me ask you this," I said, waiting for him to gesture for me to continue.

"How many nonmagicals has this office hired over the years?"

"That's not got anything to do with you," he began, but I cut him off.

"That's not true, Cary. The answer is none, isn't it?" I forced the question again.

He sighed. "Listen, Owen, you should speak to the partners; have them explain..."

I laughed. "No, they'd just want to talk me out of what I want to do. I'm going home to Illinois, and I realize I probably need some protection to keep Damian safe. I don't want to work at a firm that hired me as a boy toy for the new wizard. It took too many years of college to get my law degree..."

"It's not that. You're making assumptions."

"Logical ones. Am I wrong? Wouldn't you make the same?"

Cary sighed. "Okay, so let's say you do this. Damian is dealing with some serious concerns with his friend missing. He's going to be distraught over your leaving. That will cause him to falter. Trust me, I get it, and no, I don't blame you, but let's not be too hasty. Let's do this," he said, and I could tell his mind was beginning to catch up with the situation. "I'll hold onto this letter. If you decide to submit it after you've had time to reconsider, I'll give it to the partners. I-I can help you get to Illinois with Mr. Stages's help. You have to clue them in with your plans to go home. As our coven leader, he'll know the witches in your region, and he'll have to be the one to make the contacts."

I nodded. He was probably telling the truth. "Okay, I'll go talk to them now but only to say I'm going to Illinois, not to officially resign. I-I just can't deal with an emotional plea to stay."

I wanted to repeat myself, to force him to understand I didn't have the energy to argue with a man so powerful, not just as a witch but as a boss, and I knew he'd try to talk me into staying.

Maybe I was just overreacting, but since finding out about the spell cast by the old wizard, I had a low-level feeling that this whole set up made me a glorified plaything for Damian.

This incident had been a wakeup call for me. I just couldn't be a plaything for someone. Not again, not after all that'd gone down with my stupid ex and certainly not after spending so much time getting my degree, moving away from Illinois, and... well, and improving my life.

"I'm going to go home and pack. Cary, I'm not needed here and haven't been since I started. The partners should be able to hire someone with the skills necessary to serve the firm's clients. That isn't going to be me. However, if you want to wait before giving it to them, that's up to you. Hopefully," I said pondering aloud, "once this has blown over, and the vipers are dealt with, I can go on with my life, get a job at a regular firm, and all that."

Cary appeared sad but at least he wasn't arguing with me.

"Okay," I said mostly to avoid acknowledging that I might be making a mistake, "I'm going now."

He stood up and hugged me, which surprised me a bit. Cary was obnoxious, but I did think he was a good friend. Maybe the only real friend I'd met since I'd gotten here. Of course, this morning, I'd have said Damian was one as well, but I'd probably been wrong all along. Damn me and my romantic sensibilities.

Chapter Thirty-Seven

DAMIAN

"Orville," I called the moment I got home.

The ghost appeared immediately. "I need help, and fast," I said.

Orville looked concerned but nodded. "Do we need to discuss this in the attic?" he asked.

"No, because I need the help of all the ghosts if I'm going to fix what's happened."

Orville's left eyebrow popped up, but he nodded for me to continue. "Molly, the woman who was here the other night, she's been abducted, and we think it might be by a gang of individuals who serve the dark. Can the ghosts search for her? I need to know what I'm up against."

Orville pondered for a few moments, then shook his head. "Mr. Richards," he said, using my surname, which was unusual and alarming at the same time. "Many of the ghosts that sought this place as a sanctuary have moved on. Your willingness to entertain the witch caused most of them to leave, at least for now. I doubt you have a strong enough presence here to do the search."

I stared at him, then shook my head. "I understand," I said, and feeling the anger rising in me, I decided it was probably best to leave well enough alone. "Orville, I won't be requiring your help then. But you should let the others know I consider this a slight against the hospitality offered by my predecessor and me. Just so you know, Owen is in jeopardy too. Not helping me is the same as not helping him."

I probably shouldn't have said that, I was just angry, but when I needed them the most, when *we* needed them most, they were unwilling to help. And for what? Because I didn't know about the relationship between witches and ghosts? That I'd invited Cary over by accident?

I didn't have time to deal with them right now. I leaped up the stairs two at a time until I reached the parchment. Despite the previous conversation and what I'd thought was me smoothing over the incident, I now had no idea what my relationship with the ghosts was, and hell, if they were holding Cary against me, who knows what could be up.

I used my staff and closed the gap Elias had created that allowed Orville into the attic. I doubted he was a foe, and likely he never would be, but right now, I needed to be careful. Molly's life and possibly others were at stake. I wouldn't be taking any chances.

I opened the parchment and touched the quill to the paper. "Elias, I need help, and it's urgent."

The writing began immediately. "Explain how I can help."

I spent the next half hour explaining to Elias what had happened. Then took another half hour explaining how the ghosts had refused to help.

"I've even blocked Orville from the attic," I admitted.

"Good," Elias said. "He has that coming. Just be aware, I've done the same in the past."

I nodded. "Thanks, it's good to have confirmation. Now, how do I deal with this?" I asked.

Elias explained several scenarios, none of them without fault. If I went in, magical guns blazing, there would be a lot of fallout. I'd lost my biggest ally for covert surveillance, and that was the ghosts.

Witches were a blunt weapon to use in a situation like this. If they got involved, the fallout could be even greater, and I knew without any doubt the entity that confronted me in Molly's apartment would sacrifice her to punish me.

When asked how he would've handled things, Elias said he wasn't even sure how he would deal with things until he was dealing with them. "You can prepare for days, but it's not until you're facing your enemy that you know how to deal with them. Magical warfare is not the same as planning battles. There are just too many variables," he'd said.

"Who do you think the man he's looking for is?" I asked, and Elias was stumped.

"It's an odd request. I can't see why he'd want Owen unless it's to hurt you as you suggested, but if you gave him over, that would show you don't have any real feelings for him. I don't think Owen is the man he wanted."

"I agree, so who is he after?"

"You should've had the witches scry for that information. Do you still have the poison you withdrew from Owen?" he asked.

"Yes, I forgot about that. I should destroy it."

"Maybe not, at least not immediately. You need the witches since wizards are not experts in divination, but they should be able to scry for you. Help you see who the vipers are searching for."

I immediately texted Cary, telling him I was headed back and that Elias had recommended they do a scrying with the stuff we got out of Owen. Then I rushed downstairs and was surprised to hear Owen in the library. I went to tell him I would be back and stopped short when I opened the pocket door and found him packing. "Um, Owen, what's going on?" I asked.

He stared at me, a frown on his face. "Damian, I'm going to go home for a while. Let things calm down here. Mr. Stages has set up a small coven from my hometown to meet me at the airport. They'll drive me back home and keep an eye on me while I'm there. Mr. Stages was pretty sure I'd be safe. The vipers have more on their plate and agenda than to worry about me."

I went over to him and put my hand on his shoulder. "I-I didn't mean I wanted to break up," I said, but Owen shook his head.

"Damian," he said and turned toward me. "We only just met, and then we were thrust together by magic. People don't move in with each other after one date. You don't have to feel bad about this not being a real thing, okay? I'm not a kid. I know how things work."

He leaned up and kissed me, just a chaste kiss on the lips, before he turned back and began packing again.

I could tell he was fighting tears, and the truth was, so was I. I didn't want to lose what we'd just started. Yeah, it was fast, and yeah, I know that was weird, but I liked him a lot. Then I thought about Molly being in danger. If these Vipers could abduct her, they wouldn't hesitate to do the same with him.

I held him for several long moments, then when I let go, I said, "We will handle this, but I'm glad you'll be safe. Owen," I said and hesitated until he looked up at me, "be safe, okay?"

He nodded, then smiled and turned to finish packing.

I rushed out the door, Molly's fate driving me, even though everything told me I shouldn't let him go. If I were a light-based wizard, even if it meant a life of loneliness, I couldn't let someone like Owen be in danger just because he was with me. For real, I had to prevent that.

I ran to the witch's office, and it felt good to work my muscles. I was so frustrated with all that was happening: Molly being abducted, and Owen attacked. Now, shit, I was losing him. I could've run for a hundred miles, given the chance.

I paused to catch my breath before going into the office. Luckily, Mrs. Patterson was waiting in the conference room for me, and Cary opened the door so I could join her. "Do you have the box?" she asked when I walked in.

I nodded as I took in the large clay bowl that seemed to be ancient. I guessed it probably was, although I didn't have time to ponder that. We needed to figure things out now.

I put my hand out, and the staff immediately appeared. Mrs. Patterson blinked a few times, and I could tell my staff made her nervous. The message that went through my mind came instantly. "That's not a bad thing." The wizards who preceded me had mostly been wary of witches, even the one witch who'd become a wizard had been leery of her counterparts. However, Mrs. Patterson was helping me, and there was no indication she was or ever would be a threat.

The little box still sat on top of the staff. "Let me begin, and when I gesture to you, dip the box into the water. Just the box, though, not your staff. Gods only know what'd happen if you did that."

I smiled, thinking she was joking, but she didn't smile back. Okay, maybe I should take this more seriously. "We need to know what they want. Who they're searching for," I said.

She nodded and began chanting. The language was Samarian. Knowledge of the ancient language had come down through my predecessors as well. The chant roughly translated to *Bring us light; bring us wisdom; bring us answers; resist the night.*

She glanced up at me and gestured toward the scrying bowl. I tipped my staff upside down and gently touched the tip to the water, then quickly pulled it back.

Images immediately began to stir. I heard Mrs. Patterson repeat the chanting, but I didn't look up. Instead, I was mesmerized by the flow of color, mostly white flowing in circles around the bowl. Finally, an image began to form, and when it settled, I wondered what the hell a horse had to do with anything. Then a voice in my head corrected me. *Re'em*.

Sure enough, I examined it closer and saw the single horn protruding from the horse's skull.

"What does this mean?" I asked, but when I glanced at Mrs. Patterson, her head was laid back, her eyes blank. "Shit," I said, and the waters immediately began to stir.

"Words are important," Elias had warned me. So, I drew out my staff again and severed the magical ties between Mrs. Patterson and the scrying bowl. I called out for Cary to bring Mr. Stages, which he did immediately.

"What happened?" the old coven leader asked, and I opened my mouth to tell him, but the words wouldn't come. *They can't know about the Re'em. No one can know.* A voice echoed in my head.

"The scrying went bad," I finally said. "She needs help."

Mr. Harrison came in behind Mr. Stages, and they began to chant while placing hands on her head. Slowly, she came to and gazed up at me. "You must save him," she whispered, then fell into a deep sleep.

Deep inside, I knew whatever caused me to hold my tongue would also keep her quiet. The knowledge of a Re'em unicorn flowed through me though. Seconds ago, I would've sworn it was just a story people told little kids at night.

Maybe it was a cartoon or a fairy tale, but no, damn it, no, it was so much more. Now that I thought about it, even the Bible had references to the powerful light beast.

My head hurt with the urgency flowing through me. Information about the Re'em unicorn, how rare it was for them to reincarnate. How dangerous it was when they did.

Finally, after several moments of information download, the final blow hit me. If the Re'em fell into the wrong hands, everything would be at risk. The entire universe would be at risk.

I suddenly had an intense need to find Owen and secure him. I had no idea how he was related to the new unicorn, but all my instincts told me he was.

"I've got to go," I said, rushing out of the office and back to the house. Unfortunately, by the time I got home, it was empty.

"Owen," I said on his voicemail when he didn't answer. "You need to stay put. I'm not sure why, but you need to come back home. I'll... I'll try to explain when you get here."

I also texted him, but he didn't return my call or text. Had he turned his phone off? My insides were twisted. I didn't know which way to turn. On the one hand, Molly was missing, and I needed to confront the vipers and get her back. On the other, my instincts were screaming about Owen. The Re'em unicorn, whatever that symbolized, was just the shitty icing on the cake. I had no idea what I was supposed to do.

Chapter Thirty-Eight

OWEN

I'D FOUND AN EARLY flight to St. Louis and barely had enough time to get to the airport. The stupid flight cost too damned much, but that was the reality of buying a ticket last minute. I managed to get to the airport and through security in time to catch the final boarding call.

Only moments after I boarded the plane, it took off. Thank goodness. I didn't have the energy to think about all I was losing by returning home. I knew it was stupid that I'd gotten so attached, not to mention how much I'd gotten caught up in all the magic shit. Not that it'd ever impact me again. I was leaving to get out of that world. Get away before the hateful powers that be used my presence to hurt Damian.

Now I was on the flight, I was sure I'd done the right thing. I cared about Damian, and our short time together did nothing to negate how amazing he was or how strongly my heart felt toward him.

I closed my eyes and sighed, drawing the attention of the man next to me. "Is everything okay?" he asked, and I opened my eyes, smiling at him.

"Yeah, just, you know, lots of life changes happening all at once."

The man regarded me a moment, then smiled. "Oh, sometimes life comes at you fast. Other times, it's slow and plodding. Why don't I read your cards?" he said.

I chuckled. "Tarot cards?" I asked, and he winked before nodding. "Um, okay, I guess."

I figured, why the hell not? It's not like I hadn't just left a city of witches and dark forces threatening to kidnap me, not to mention what they were doing to Damian's friend Molly. Or for that matter the damn wizard I was sure I'd fallen in love with.

The guy certainly looked the part. He was dark, brooding, and wore clothes like he was trying to be steampunk or something. White shirt, black bow tie, black vest, long black coat, black pants. He even wore a freaking black top hat and a cane. No idea how he got that through security.

He winked as he pulled a box of cards out of his bag, lowered the seat tray, and began shuffling.

He chatted about the type of deck he was using, saying it was an original design and telling the story of the woman who'd painted the cards, giving me a history lesson. At one point, I lost interest and waited while he shuffled and spread the cards out in front of him. "Here, lower your tray, then pick one of the cards and flip it onto its back, revealing which card is yours."

I stared at the cards, hesitating, then chose one at random. I tugged the card out and was about to turn it over when I realized two cards had stuck together. I rubbed them together until they separated, then showed the guy what had happened.

"Now, that's strange," he said as he examined the cards. "How did that one get in there?" he asked, pointing at a decorative card under the more traditional one. "Might as well turn them both over."

I flipped over the one with the unicorn on the back first and then the other one. Of course, now I was convinced the man had planted them. They were both the same card—the Wheel of Fortune.

"Well, I'll be," he said, examining the cards. "You know, I...I haven't had that deck in years. I gave the unicorn deck away in the late nineties. I have no idea how that got in there, but let's look at the cards. Do you know what the Wheel of Fortune means?" he asked, and I shook my head. I didn't want to tell him that until recently, I thought it was all a bunch of bull.

"Where one journey ends, another begins. See the snake? The viper is a dark entity, representing all that's evil, but the wheel turns, good or bad. The unicorn on this card and Anubis on this one both represent the good. Bad or good, things will always change. I'm guessing your life is changing. Is it not?" he asked and I nodded, and before I could stop it a fat tear ran down my face.

"I... Yeah, even if I'm not ready for it."

He patted my hand and collected the Wheel of Fortune from my tray. "You hold onto that card, the one with the unicorn. I loved that deck, and I'm guessing this is a message to find and replace those in my collection. For you, it is a great symbol. Who knows, that card could be a good omen."

"Maybe," I said as I tucked the card into my coat pocket. We spent most of the flight talking about my time back in Seattle and the law firm I'd worked at. I told him everything about myself without going into detail about my brief relationship being with a wizard and my job working for witches.

"Life is short, young man. You have to take advantage of love when it presents itself. Don't be afraid to embrace it, even when it comes at you fast," he said just as the plane began its descent into St. Louis.

I was surprised how fast the flight had gone. I was afraid the time would drag, considering I'd just left a life I'd been so happy with a few hours ago. The man wished me luck, and when he winked, a real light twinkled in his eye. I almost felt nervous that I had sat with another magical person the entire time, but I knew he wasn't dangerous. Besides, he disappeared right after we landed, and I didn't see him again.

I came out of security to the baggage claim to find a somewhat wilted older couple holding a sign with my name. "Hi, I'm Owen," I said, and the couple smiled.

"We've been sent to pick you up. We're parked outside. I felt bad about such an elderly couple picking me up, but if they were witches, I had to assume they could take care of themselves. Luckily, my bag rolled around, so I grabbed it and followed them to their car and back to the town I'd left just months before with the hope of a new and brighter future.

Oh well, at least I'd connected with new and fascinating people before my life fell apart. That's something I'd remember for the rest of my life. Not that this life would give me much to look forward to.

CHAPTER THIRTY-NINE

DAMIAN

"How safe is it to ask questions across the veil?" I asked the parchment.

"I'm sure it's just you and me. The parchment is ancient, but it's imbedded with my blood, my DNA, and those who have preceded me. It should be very safe."

"The Re'em unicorn has returned," I said and was suddenly very happy Orville could no longer come up to the attic.

Elias, via the parchment, didn't respond for several long moments. Finally, he said, "The arrival of the Re'em brings about two things. First, historically, it represents purity and can cleanse even the most impure. Second, the Re'em is vulnerable, at least in its formative years. Once it's fully powerful, of course, nothing can harm it. But it is intensely vulnerable at the beginning of its life.

"The Re'em itself is a correction. When the balance on Earth tips too far to the dark, the unicorn is released to bring balance back. If those who wish to tip the scales irrevocably can get ahold of the unicorn before it has developed its powers and strength, they can throw the universe into darkness that may take centuries to overcome."

"Can you explain?" I asked, and Elias paused before clarifying.

"Yes, we've experienced such anomalies in history. Europe's Middle Ages were the last. It took a very long time for us to crawl out of those years, and we almost failed. Think of the plagues that swept across the earth.

The destruction in the last few centuries is still related to the problems of the previous two millennia. The Re'em's blood was spilled, and darkness swept in behind it.

If a unicorn has returned, you must do everything in your power to protect it. Give it time and space to mature so it can heal the earth. As the Legacy Wizard, it would be your job and responsibility. Nothing would be more important.

I didn't dare tell him I saw Owen in those images. That he was possibly the Re'em unicorn. I hadn't accepted that at first, not until I'd begun talking to Elias.

Now, it was clear and I couldn't help but tremble at the thought that the vipers had somehow figured out who or what he was. I needed to find him fast. I smiled as my thoughts drifted to an idea."

"Elias, I may need your help. Can you help me create a golem?"

"Golems aren't of the light, wizard."

"They aren't of the darkness either, if my instincts are correct. I need it to protect the Re'em."

"I can help, but you must put spells on the golem to ensure it doesn't harm the innocent. Yet, if this is what you need to protect the Re'em, you should do it."

I followed Elias's directions on which substances I needed for the golem. I needed to create it using the light. Not only because of the oath I intrinsically made as a Legacy Wizard, but if the vipers knew or even suspected what Owen was, the golem must not give off any dark. Something I should've noticed about Owen was that he was pure light. Jeez, I let so much get past me. Being a new wizard wasn't a good enough excuse.

When I went downstairs to find something with Owen's DNA, I ran into four very concerned-looking ghosts. "Is Owen okay?" Lucious asked.

I stared at them and had to force down my anger. "Do any of you care? When I asked for help earlier…"

Orville interrupted me. "When you asked earlier, I was upset because several of our occupants had just left. I acted inappropriately. You have our help, we will do anything to protect Owen."

I ignored them while searching for what I needed, and when I found a strand of hair, I headed back upstairs. "If you really want to help, you'll find out where Molly and any of her friends are. I'm going to try to protect Owen, but I need to save them too."

I was about to go back upstairs but stopped and turned around on the first step. "I know my predecessor opened his house to you before I came here. I've also honored his wishes. Owen and I screwed up by not understanding your relationship with the witches and inviting one in, but you've seriously damaged my trust." I paused and then sighed. "Don't get me wrong, I would never do anything to sever our relationship, but relationships are two-way streets. It can't just be me and Owen allowing you to stay here, then you get mad and turn your backs on us."

All four ghosts nodded, and I looked at Orville as he made eye contact. "I'm sorry, Damian," he said.

"We all are," Lucious added.

"Okay, I'm going to be busy for the next day or so. If you can find out where the vipers, a gang on the east side of town, are hiding Molly and anyone else they've captured, and how many they've captured, that would help more than anything else."

All four nodded, and I turned, smiling. I did understand why they had gotten angry. I'm sure I would've too, but it felt good that they had our backs, especially when Owen was so vulnerable. If we were lucky, I could use the golem to get Molly and the others back.

Then, I'd do what I could to protect him. However, my golem would need to survive at least a week if my plan to save and protect Owen worked. Gods help us all if it didn't.

Chapter Forty

OWEN

B Y THE TIME THE elderly witches dropped me off at my
mother's house with a promise to keep the perimeter
guarded, I could tell they were tired. I had no idea how they
were going to keep me under surveillance when they were so
clearly ready for their bed.

I didn't think it mattered that much though. I doubted the
Vipers or anyone else would be seeking me here. I thanked the
two profusely, then rushed into Mom's house.

Chloe, Mom's little Yorkie, met me at the door, and I
scooped her up and kissed her, then went to put her out back
so she could do her business. When I rounded the corner, I
stopped short when Eric Strange stood arrogantly smiling at
me.

"Well, the prodigal son returns home, I see."

"Eric, I didn't think Mom had anyone over," I said.

"Your mother left this morning and asked me to let Chloe
out. Never fear, I was just about to leave."

I nodded, went to the back door, opened it, and let the little Yorkie out. When I turned around, Eric had gone. I listened and sighed when I heard the front door shut. "Just great," I said, "perfect greeting party."

Chloe finished peeing, which, of course, had the jerk let her out, she wouldn't have needed to go, and I let her back in. It was late, later than she usually ate, but I had to assume if he hadn't let her out, he probably hadn't fed her either, so I pulled out the fancy dog food Mom insisted on buying and filled her dish.

Sure enough, she went right for it. Chloe wasn't one to overeat, so the asshole certainly hadn't done anything. It just made me wonder why he'd come over. Most likely to rub it in my face that he was here, and I wasn't.

Oh well, no use worrying about the bully ex. He was firmly in my past. I didn't have the energy to be dealing with him.

I grabbed my phone and texted my mother.

> Me: Eric Strange was here, said he was taking care of Chloe. Just so you know, he wasn't doing a good job.

Truth was, I probably texted that just to be an ass. Mom shouldn't have put me in a position to face my fucking ex like that. Even if she was angry that I'd moved away.

I went upstairs, leaving my phone on the countertop. I was trying to figure out whether I should unpack or not. Maybe I should just leave my shit in my bag until I knew what I was doing. Seeing Eric was enough to remind me I wasn't really welcome here. It might've been my home once, but it certainly wasn't now.

At least it did give me a refuge for the moment.

I lay on my bed, closed my eyes, and immediately remembered the card in my shirt pocket. I removed it and studied the symbols. Light and dark. The spinning of the wheel. That certainly described my life.

Even seeing my stupid ex. Whether or not Damian wanted to be with me any longer, he was a bright light compared to Eric's darkness. *At least*, I thought as I fell asleep, *I'd done a better job with the last ex than with my first.*

Chapter Forty-One

DAMIAN

Making the golem was unpleasant, and I could understand why Elias said it wasn't of the light. It felt off to create such a creature, but since I wasn't using my powers as a wizard, it wasn't like I was doing dark magic.

Golems themselves were benign. Made of the earth, in most ways, they weren't much different from humans. I think the neutral energy required to create it was the only thing that saved me from doing the dark's bidding.

I collected the clay just as the day broke. I knew instinctively where to find it. Luckily, a store just around the corner from where I lived stocked it. I wouldn't have to dig this particular clay up from the ground.

As soon as the sun set, I began to form the man. Feet first, then the mouth and head. I slipped in the parchment required for the act. Luckily, Elias had stored a few sheets in one of the drawers in the attic for a spell such as this one.

I wrote the appropriate message, then slipped it into the mouth, chanting the words necessary to activate the spell. I waited to see if my powers rebelled, and when they didn't, I left the golem lying on my dining table and went into the backyard. There had been three people buried here. Long ago, before the houses had been built. Luckily, none of them were the spirits that occupied the house, but when I'd searched internally for a graveyard near me, I'd felt the graves. Luckily, that's all I could say because the spell required a good chunk of graveyard dirt that sat above the long-decayed corpses beneath.

I rushed back into the dining room and spread the grave dirt around the golem, something I knew instinctively to do.

I applied Owen's hair to the head and wrote the words to animate it. "You will become a proxy for Owen Lloyd, you will have his memories, you will be like him and will not know that you aren't. You will serve until Owen is safe and the darkness threatening him is dispelled."

I cut my palm and let the blood drip into the golem's mouth and onto the parchment. I felt dizzy but knew that was part of it. I was putting my DNA, my life force, into the being. Luckily, it was not enough to be afraid but certainly enough to be reticent. The golem would be a powerful tool, but one that could do damage as well.

Before the golem was animated, I placed an X over its heart. "With harm to none, so I will it be. With good and light, you will provide service for me!"

I placed my still bloodied hand over its forehead, then said, "Wake, golem. Wake and take your form."

The clay figure didn't move at first, but then I saw it twitch. Its eyes opened first and slowly transformed from clay to the eyes I recognized as Owen's.

The rest of him formed, one feature after another, until it appeared my beloved Owen was lying on the table. "Are you aware?" I asked, and he nodded. "And do you know your mission?"

"I'm a proxy for Owen Lloyd. I'm to protect him if I can."

"You are ready," I said, then stood back. I wrapped my hand, knowing I couldn't use my powers to heal myself, although I knew intuitively that would happen before morning anyway. I sat with the golem and questioned him, and when morning finally broke, I was confident the golem was enough of a stand-in for me to get my friends back.

I called Cary and told him to meet us at the café we'd met at before. Might as well do what we could to expose this golem and see if he was up to the task. If he couldn't fool Cary, he wouldn't fool the vipers either.

When Cary saw Owen, he gasped. "You're back? Owen, what's going on?"

The golem sighed and, just like Owen would've done, flopped down into his seat. "I... Cary, it's all too much."

Cary reached over and took Owen's hand. "I'm glad I didn't submit that letter of resignation. Can you come back to the office today? I know the partners are worried about you."

The golem chewed on his lip for a moment, then nodded. "Yes, I can come in."

I watched Cary, and when the two of them left, the wave of relief that washed over me was almost indescribable. Maybe now, provided they didn't get wind of where Owen actually was, I'd have time to do all I needed to do.

I walked into Molly's apartment and sent magic into the few remaining connections between the vipers and this space. *"So, you've changed your mind?"* the disembodied voice asked.

"Who do you want? I need specifics."

"You know who we want and why. If you don't, then you are a piss-poor wizard."

Images came to my mind, a man who'd dated Shadow a few months ago. He was short and a little pudgy, not who you'd expect someone like Shadow to date. Now I knew who was behind the disembodied voice from before, that would help me in the future.

"There are conditions if you want to trade."

The man laughed. *"I don't think you have the power to negotiate."*

"I have the light source. You have a couple of wannabe witches. I think I'm the one with the power here."

That shut the idiot up. I just hoped he didn't have more than two people.

"I'm restricting how much energy you can pull from the light source. He has to choose to go with you too. It can't be me giving him to you. I will allow him to be taken, allow him to make the choice, but if I don't see my friends released, I will blow you and your little club to ashes, and you know I can do that, do you not, viper?" I asked and spread the name of the gang out like it was the most disgusting thing I've ever said.

He was silent, and I got the feeling he was talking to someone. *"Shadow will not come with you. She is committed to me, but your friend, Molly, will be released as soon as the light source is taken."*

The way he said light source, I had to assume he didn't know exactly what Owen was. That was good. Shadow—she was one of them. That helped, so I didn't have to worry about her. Of course, they could be lying. My gut told me Molly would be able to shed some interesting light on this question though. We just had to get her back.

I left Molly's apartment, then cast a spell that hid me from all creatures, both the dark and light. It was a powerful spell most magical creatures had no idea wizards could cast. With my staff, I could maintain my invisibility indefinitely, which for now, I needed.

My first stop was the house, where I summoned Orville and found out we'd been correct, and Molly and Shadow were both with the vipers. Molly was the only one who was bound. Although Orville said she appeared concerned and kept going back to check on Molly, Shadow was definitely part of the group who'd kidnapped her.

I went to Owen's law office after asking Orville to let the ghosts know I would attempt to rescue Molly that afternoon and planned to follow the vipers to their lair tonight if they took the bait.

I stayed well out of range of the law office. I had faith in the cloak, but the witches there had known my predecessor and were themselves very powerful. It was better to be safe than sorry and stay on this side of the street.

At five, Owen and Cary came out of the office, and I could tell Cary would accompany Owen back to my house, which I'd planned for too. I picked up the phone, called the office, and asked for Cary to be called back so I could tell him something important.

Mrs. Patterson showed up before they could get to Cary's car and pulled him back, leaving Owen's golem standing vulnerable as I'd hoped. "Hello?" Cary answered.

"You will have to trust me, Cary. Don't go back outside. Owen is safe, but the vipers are about to take him."

"What? No, I won't let you..."

"Cary, there is no other choice, and Owen is not in danger. I swear on my honor and word as the Legacy Wizard. Do you understand?"

Just then, a van swerved into an empty space in front of Owen's golem, and I smiled as they pulled him into the vehicle before disappearing down the road.

"Okay, the trap's been set. Please stay close to your phone, if I call, answer. I-I might need your help to pull this off."

Cary made a noncommitted okay, but I couldn't linger. I needed to follow the van. I closed my eyes and magically caught a ride in the wake of the van. It was a strange spell that almost caused me to lose the cloak, but my staff was powerful enough to maintain the two massive energy-sucking spells.

It only took fifteen minutes for us to arrive at the viper's lair. Owen was pulled out of the van, and they were about to take him inside when I magically stopped them in their tracks. "Come out, come out!" I called as I walked up to where I'd frozen the men and the golem.

A moment later, the man I'd recognized in the vision came out smiling. "What an honor to meet the great Legacy Wizard," he said and bowed ironically.

"Honor your agreement, or I will honor mine."

"Now, now, there's no need for such aggression. Bring out the girl," he yelled, and a moment later, Shadow came out, pushing Molly in front of her.

"Now," he said, not even glancing back at where my friend stood, looking the worse for wear. Luckily, the fog that covered her eyes told me she was in a trance. "Owen, dear boy, if you'll agree to spend some quality time with me, I will be happy to let your little friend here go."

The golem turned toward me, and I nodded. "I will stay."

"Before he does, show me your sign. Can you be trusted, witch?" I asked.

The man laughed. "So demanding." He lifted his hand, a wand appeared, and he sent the light toward me. Usually, when two magical beings made an agreement, they did so with a gentle light exchange. There was nothing gentle about this one. However, I lifted my hand and let the dark light absorb into my palm as my own light flowed out and into his.

"Owen, if you need me, just call."

"Oh, that won't be necessary. We will treat our guest with the utmost respect, won't we?" he said and then slapped Shadow on the ass.

The look she gave him was pure hatred, and that made me feel a little better. Maybe it wasn't all her idea after all.

I watched as they released Molly and took the golem into the building behind them, leaving Molly and me standing outside. I rushed to her and, using my powers, transferred us back to my house with a wave of my staff. Thank the gods for the staff. With all the energy I was expending, I'd be dead if I were using my own. I was just about to walk her through the gate when all the alarms sounded in my head.

They'd tagged her. Shit, I couldn't take her in without jeopardizing my own wards. I grabbed my phone and called Cary. "I need to bring Molly over to your office. I can't take her into my house without destroying the wards I've built there. She's been tagged with more energy than I can remove alone."

"No, not the office," he said. "Bring her to Mt. Pleasant Cemetery. I'll ask Mr. Stages to have the coven meet you there."

"Thanks, Cary, we'll head there now."

I had no choice but to leave Molly standing outside the gate, but I surrounded her with enough magic to kill anything living that might try to take her. I rushed in, got the car from the garage, and called Orville while backing out.

He showed up and looked perplexed. "It worked. I have Molly, but we have to remove the poison in her system. Do you have spirits still spying on the vipers?" I asked, and he nodded. "Good, I'll need a full report when I get back. I'll go get Owen."

He patted my back and disappeared as I pulled out of the property. Molly was still standing where I'd left her, so I jumped out, put her into the back seat, and rushed to the ancient cemetery to meet the witches and, hopefully, save my friend's life.

Chapter Forty-Two

OWEN

NIGHTMARES FILLED MY HEAD as I slept. I was a horse running in the dark, and something was chasing me. Something behind me. I ran as fast as I could, and then I was ensnared in a trap, my legs tangled, and I was falling to the earth.

I was paralyzed, unable to move, unable to scream for help. Then I looked up and into the face of Eric Strange. His face was grotesquely warped, and there was madness in his eyes. He drew a knife, the scary curved ones like you see in old movies about Alexander the Great. He rose into the air and laughed maniacally as he brought the knife down, ending my life.

I woke with a start and eyed the space, terrified. Where was I? Finally, it came to me, I was home, back in my old bedroom. I wandered down to the kitchen, where Chloe was waiting to go outside.

"Okay, girl, give me just a moment," I said, grabbing my phone before letting the little dog out to do her business.

I checked my phone and saw I had a message from Mom.

> Her: Eric shouldn't have been in my
> house. No one should've. I'm calling him
> now. Don't let him back in.

The dream came back to me, the horse running and getting trapped, only to be slaughtered by the creepy-looking Eric Strange.

I shuddered at the thought and was happy when Chloe darted back into the house, begging for her evening treat.

If I'd learned one thing living with witches and wizards it was that you don't ignore dreams, especially when they were as vivid as that.

I dialed Cary, and when he didn't answer, I left a message. "Hey, Cary, um, I had a weird dream. I was a horse running through a forest and got tangled in a snare. My ex was there and ended up killing me. I know that sounds weird, but you know, magic and stuff, it seemed important. Oh, and by the way, that boyfriend was here at my mom's house when I got home. Mom said he shouldn't have been here, so that could be what was behind it. Just thought I'd better be safe than sorry."

I hung up, and not knowing what else to do, I grabbed some of my mom's sage from her spice cabinet and started a fire in the fireplace. I tossed the sage in front of the logs, knowing at least some of the smoke would come into the room.

Maybe that would help me chase off the negative thoughts, if not the entities themselves. I was afraid. I knew I probably shouldn't be. Eric was creepy, and being in Mom's house was freaky in every sense of the word, but he wasn't magical. At least, I didn't think he was. I pondered calling out to the witches assigned to be with me but figured I was being paranoid. I'd learned there was magic in the world and now I was seeing it everywhere.

Mom had probably told him I was coming home, and he wanted to gloat. Regardless, he'd freaked me out enough that I'd had that dream. "Ugh," I told the room and scooped Chloe up. After checking to make sure all the doors were locked, I went back upstairs and drew a nice bath in Mom's jacuzzi tub. I needed a little relaxation, especially after that dream.

Chloe went to her bed next to Mom's, and I climbed into the tub, letting the bubbles and jets relax my nerves. I couldn't help but compare Eric to Damian. Damian was so sweet, so loving.

Yeah, I'd only known him briefly, and truth was, I had misjudged Eric back then, assuming he was a good guy. But I have to admit, I knew he wasn't. Now, I could admit to myself, as I lay in the tub staring at the ceiling, that I had known Eric was a player.

I had been a lonely little gay boy in the middle of nowhere, Illinois. When Eric showed interest, it made me happy. It sorta gave me validation. Hindsight's twenty-twenty, though, and now I knew him for what he was. Now, I had come to terms with it.

Damian wasn't anything like Eric. I could say that without feeling concerned that I'd missed something. Although it didn't matter, Damian was through with me. I know he said he wasn't, but if he wanted me, like I will admit I wanted him, he'd have fought, right?

"I could've fought for him too," I said to the bathroom and laughed. "I need to fight for him."

The revelation hit me like a ton of bricks. I'd just given up and walked out, feeling sorry for myself instead of fighting for him, fighting for my life. A life I loved even if I'd only had a short time to accept how much I'd loved it.

I got up, dried off, and pulled my sweatpants and shirt on. Mom's old house was always drafty, so I also pulled on a pair of thick socks I kept in my top drawer. It wasn't something I'd want anyone to ever see me in. I always thought I looked like a giant gray turd in my sweats, but damn it, Illinois was fucking cold in the winter.

I chuckled as I went to my bedroom and checked my phone. No call or text from Cary. Hopefully, that meant he wasn't on a hot date or something. I shook off the feeling that something wasn't right. I'd clearly spent too much time in the care of the magical. I was letting it get the better of me.

Hell, I'd grown up in this house and this town. The witches that'd come to get me were ancient. There was clearly no threat here, just as I'd assumed there wouldn't be.

I put my phone on the charger and walked downstairs right into a trap, like the one I'd visualized a couple of hours before in my dream.

CHAPTER FORTY-THREE

DAMIAN

T HE CEMETERY WAS CREEPY, and I lived with ghosts. Knowing this was where the witches practiced their craft should've made me feel less creeped out because no spirits would be lingering here.

I soon realized it wasn't the fear of spirits that had caused me to dislike the cemetery, rather it was the intensity of the magic that permeated the ground here. It wasn't natural, and that bothered my need for balance. That's something I'd need to discuss with Elias later.

The witches met us at the arched entrance and took charge of Molly. I could tell they would've preferred I didn't go in, but no one complained when I followed Molly as they led her into the darkened cemetery.

A large group of witches formed a circle surrounding a pergola-like mausoleum. When we got to the center, I noticed a large stone on the ground. I knew it was a grave, but my senses told me the corpse had long ago returned to the earth.

I could tell the occupant had been a witch, therefore it made sense the coven met here. They laid Molly on the slab, and I immediately understood what kind of spell they were casting.

The tag on Owen had been small, but it still took a lot of magic to remove it. Molly had been inundated with similar tags, and the poison flowed freely through her veins. If it wasn't removed soon, she would die.

I stood back, sat on a bench not far from the slab, and watched as the witches called upon the earth to lift and cleanse her body. It wasn't literal, thank goodness, as I didn't know how I'd feel about my friend being pulled into a grave. Then they called on fire, water, and finally air.

I felt the shift in energy as each element was called. This was ancient magic, strong because of its age. Stronger still as it pulled from the very foundation of our planet. Not even the intensity of the tags within Molly could resist that level of power and magic.

Half an hour after the spellcasting began, I realized Molly would be fine. Thank the gods, she was going to be okay.

I felt the spell ending and stood, drawing my staff so that when the witches turned toward me, I could bless them for what they'd done. Molly had used dark magic, it was clear she would've had to, or she wouldn't have been so tightly wrapped in their poison.

The witches had been her only hope, and they'd done this for me. They had saved my best friend not because they owed me or wanted something from me. They'd done it because I'd asked, plain and simple.

Cary lifted Molly onto her feet and let her lean on him as they walked toward me. The entire Coven seemed to have noticed me at the same time and, like a well-choreographed dance, stopped all at once, causing me to chuckle silently.

"You have honored me tonight by saving one who light was no longer allowed to touch—someone who means a great deal to me. I will offer you this blessing as a gift for your unconditional willingness to help."

I lifted my staff, and light flew from the bottom into the graveyard, solidifying and balancing the powers there. With the balance came a promise that whatever they had here wouldn't be able to be taken away.

I knew the imbalance was possibly part of its desirability, but as the Legacy Wizard, they all knew I wouldn't be able to tolerate it. It was a compromise and a real gift. From now on, this would be sacred ground, and not even the Legacy Wizards who followed me could undo their claim.

As the power flowed through the ground, it reached up into each of the witches, and although I hadn't anticipated that, each of them received a small amount of the magic the place bestowed. Oops, I thought. I had inadvertently turned them all a little more toward the light. I hoped they all saw that as a gift. I certainly meant it to be.

Cary came forward with Molly and was about to hand her to me when my heart felt like someone had stuck a knife in it. I crumpled, grasping at my chest.

"Damian," Cary said, and I could hear concern in his voice. "Damian, are you okay?"

"No, no, something's happened to Owen!"

"Damn," Mr. Stages said. "I knew you shouldn't have trusted those degenerates with that boy."

I shook my head. "I didn't. The one the vipers have is a golem. The real Owen was supposed to be safe in his hometown."

Mrs. Patterson came up and laid her hand on my shoulder. "Damian," she whispered and helped me stand. "If the boy's been attacked, you know how dangerous that is. Let us help you rescue him, there might not be time to wait."

I looked into the old witch's eyes and nodded, knowing she understood as well as I did how dangerous Owen's capture, the capture of the Re'em unicorn, would be for our world.

"I used my staff and encircled the little group, Molly included, with a bubble of security. To be safe, I whispered, "The Re'em unicorn has returned, and he is our own Owen. We must rescue him, or horrible things will happen."

Chapter Forty-Four

OWEN

I couldn't move. How the hell was I standing in the middle of my mom's kitchen and completely unable to move? Magic, fucking magic. That's how!

It was like quicksand. The harder I struggled, the tighter the invisible strands held me. Luckily, I'd left Chloe upstairs and realized instinct must've been driving me.

The front door opened. Mom's open floor plan let me see exactly who my captor was. Eric Strange strode into the house, smiling like he'd just won the lottery. Maybe, if my suspicions were correct, he had.

"Well, well, how you've changed," Eric said as he strode toward me. I wanted to cuss the son of a bitch out, but one of the strands had forced my mouth shut, so all I could do was yell at him with my mouth closed. He chuckled as he walked around me, looking me up and down like I was some prized stallion or something.

"I can't believe I missed it. You weren't showing, though. You hid your real identity well, that's for sure." I stared at him. What the hell was he talking about? "You almost slipped out of my hands too. Now that really would've been a shame. As it is, you'll fetch a nice price and put me higher in the organization," he said. The idiot had finally lost his mind. Not that he had much of one to begin with.

Okay, maybe that's not entirely true. Eric was a lot of things, but dumb wasn't one of them.

"Mm mm mo," I said, and hoped he understood me saying let me go.

He just laughed. "Not likely, not as valuable as you are, but I can make you a little more comfortable as long as you don't try to run away."

I stared at him with as mean a look as I could. God, help me, as soon as I was free, I was going to knock this asshole into next week. Not that I could hit very well, or at least I've never tried, but there's a time for everything.

Eric wove his hand around my head, and the bonds began to ease, confirming the jerk did have powers. How was it that I've dated only two men, and both were magical? At least Damian was decent, unlike this asshole.

"What the hell are you doing?" I asked as soon as I could speak.

"I'm going to give you to Balthazar, of course,"

"Who? Eric, stop this nonsense and let me go."

Eric held onto the island and laughed out loud. "You are funny. Now, tell me, how did you hide all this?" he asked as he waved his hands up and down, indicating me.

"Hide what? You're so full of crap,"

"Yet, you aren't surprised by my powers, are you?" he asked, and I realized he had me there.

"No, I ran into real witches in Seattle. I know all about this weird magical world you're in." I intentionally left out that I'd dated a prominent wizard. I hoped this was some weird ruse, not a ploy to get at Damian.

"Witches, you say, and I assume they were of the light, were they not?"

"Of course, they were. Why would I hang out with the dark?"

"Aah, so you do know?"

"Know what, you nincompoop? That I have no magical powers whatsoever and that my ex-boyfriend is a total jackass? I already knew that!"

Eric stared at me, then walked over to the far wall where Mom had an ugly gold mirror, which I'd always hated, and brought it over to me. "Look!" he demanded.

When I did, I saw my image transform. I became a horse, then...a fucking unicorn? "For Pete's sake, stop the ridiculousness. You're trying to tell me I'm a unicorn? Eric, let me go!" I demanded.

He considered me for a while before hanging the mirror back up. "You truly don't realize what you are, even after I've shown you."

"Listen, this whole magic thing is new to me. I don't get it. I don't want to get it. I do know you can make that mirror show what you want. So, before you ask, I won't get back together with you. You're an asshole who screwed me, then forced me to flee my own home."

Eric's eyebrow rose like I amused him, but he didn't try to stop my tirade. Good, if I could convince him to leave me alone, I could get the fuck out.

"I don't have powers. I know I don't have powers. I'm not a fucking unicorn because they don't exist. I think I'd know if I were, don't you?" I asked. "Now, let me go!" Eric surprised me by waving his hand and releasing the bonds. "Thank you. Now get the fuck out."

Eric's expression changed, and he began stalking me. His face sent shivers up my spine. I knew I was in danger, and I quickly backed away. I was just about to turn and rush up the stairs when Eric sped across the kitchen, catching me and biting my neck.

"Ouch, what the fuck!" I yelled.

Eric pulled back, and for fuck's sake, he had the fangs of a damned vampire. A fucking vampire. Well, that explained a lot, considering he'd just bitten my neck.

I pushed him back and put my hand to my neck. "I'd better not turn into a damned vampire, Eric. God help me, if I do, I'm going to kill you!"

I waited for him to make a snarky comment, but instead, his eyes turned milky, and he began to convulse. "Fuck!" I said as I spied my phone on the counter. I rushed forward, grabbed it, and ran out the front door. The second I got outside, I saw the carnage.

The two elderly witches who'd been assigned to keep vigil over me were dead, their bodies mangled. "Fuck, fuck!" I kept saying as I rushed for my mom's car.

I managed to get inside and found the key she kept hidden under the seat. Mom was paranoid, so she kept a key in the car. I had just cranked the engine when the vehicle lifted off the ground.

"Oh no, my tasty morsel," Eric said, and even though the doors and windows were closed, I could still hear him like he was inside the car with me. "You aren't going anywhere, and I'll have more of your blood before Balthazar comes to collect you. You are one tasty, tasty Re'em!"

I remembered my phone and, not sure what would happen next, I texted Damian.

> Me: I'm in trouble. My ex is a vampire and has captured me. Help me if you can!

I didn't have time to wait for his reply before the car landed with a jarring thud, and the driver's door was ripped from its hinges.

"Now, come to me, and let me taste you again!"

CHAPTER FORTY-FIVE

DAMIAN

FEAR COURSED THROUGH ME. I could feel every moment ticking closer and closer to something horrible happening to Owen.

"Damian, focus," Cary said.

I turned to him and saw the same alarm in his expression. "What...what do I do?"

"Focus," Cary said again. "You're the Legacy Wizard. Your skills are innate. Look inside. You're letting your fears block your abilities and putting Owen at further risk!"

That snapped me back into a sound state of mind, so I closed my eyes and let the thoughts come to me. I saw him at home. I thought the house was modern and renovated because I could feel the essence of the place. I focused on trying to see him, but he wasn't inside. Something was blocking me from seeing him, even though I could feel he'd been here not long ago.

"I can see where he's been, but he's not there now. He's not safe! I-I think he's been captured."

My phone dinged, but I didn't dare take my eyes off the visions. "We need to get to him now!" I said, and my intuition kicked in, giving me the know-how regarding teleportation that would be required to get me from here to there.

"I-I'm going to teleport to Illinois. I need to get to him."

"Not yet," Mr. Stages said, and I turned toward him about to argue. "You can't rush into that situation. It could be a trap set for you as much as for him. Can you tell us what kind of magical person or creature has him?"

I nodded and closed my eyes. This time, I let my intuition guide me through the home, trying to detect magical energies. I immediately saw the exhausted magic that had been used to bind him. The ropelike structures were still lying on the ground. In my vision, I went toward them and stopped. "These were made by something very powerful. Too powerful," I said, knowing everyone could hear me.

I reached out with my powers, and the moment they collided with the bonds, I felt it. "Balthazar. These were created by Balthazar himself, but there's more here." The other power source was much weaker, almost undetectable, but as I moved toward the stairs, I caught a whiff of blood. Owen's blood. "Fuck," I said out loud and could hear both Mrs. Patterson and Mr. Stages suck in air and knew they wanted to chastise me for using such language.

"It's a vampire," I said, opening my eyes. "And it's already attacked Owen!"

"Ugh, of course it is," Cary said. "I hate vampires so much."

"I searched my intuition for details but couldn't feel much. "What? What about them? I-I can't see it or them."

"They aren't technically magical creatures," Mr. Harrison said. "They're more of a spell gone wrong, very wrong."

"Regardless, drinking the Re'em's blood will make it stronger, at least at first. If it takes from Owen often, though, his blood will kill it, so there's some consolation."

"I don't want it sucking Owen's blood at all, okay? So I'm guessing this means I need help. Will you come with me?" I asked.

Just then, my staff appeared, pulling my hand upward as it did. The little cube Mr. Stages had given me floating out of the top.

Mr. Stages just laughed. "You don't have to claim that yet, even though your staff is correct. I have already pledged our support, but keep that. I can feel there will be a time when you'll need our support again, and I might not always be the leader. For now, *our* Owen is in danger. We are already committed to saving him. He is one of our own, after all."

I could've cried. I needed their help because I was so green and had much more to learn before taking on such a serious foe. Balthazar was a dangerous enemy. He'd been reincarnating himself since the Middle Ages, creating chaos and hoping to unbalance the universe permanently. Balthazar increased his powers through chaos. The more unbalanced the universe, the more powerful he grew.

"Okay, luckily, Balthazar doesn't have him. I know that much. I suspect the vampire is doing his bidding, but we need to go now!" I said, and Molly answered, her voice quiet.

"Damian? I-I don't understand any of this," she said, glancing around the circle, but how can I help? Poor Owen." I could see emotion welling up inside her.

I studied her, looking for how deep the darkness inside her was. It wasn't thick, which meant she hadn't done anything horrible, just participated in a spell or something. Enough that the light entities wouldn't help her, enough that I couldn't do much for her either.

"I...you're at risk too. I can't do much to keep you safe until we cleanse your aura," I said, and my mind began to go to the occupants of my home. "Cary, the spirits in my home hate you, but I think if you and Molly go together, you can rally their support. However," I said quickly to ensure I didn't overstep, "I need a vow that none of you will try to cross over any spirits who help us tonight."

I saw how that hit. Witches firmly believed that ghosts should be crossed over, which had become clearer over the past weeks since Cary had come to visit. However, I didn't entirely agree. Ghosts should have agency as much as the living. If they weren't harming others, they should be allowed to live in this realm unmolested.

I waited several anxious moments as I saw the witches considering my request. "It goes against our vows. It's too much to ask," Mr. Stages said.

"I can't in good conscience ask my allies to help if it puts them in danger from my other allies. At the very least, can you agree not to go against the ghosts residing in my home until the mission is complete?" I asked.

Mr. Stages turned toward Mr. Harrison and then Mrs. Patterson, and all three nodded. "You've got our vow to refrain from acting against the spirits under your care, at least while they are in your service, but this agreement is negated if any of them allow their energies to be used by the dark forces. Sorcery is our greatest enemy and an enemy of the balance between dark and light. It can't be tolerated!"

"Agreed," I said, lifting my hand to initiate the agreement. Mr. Stages raised his, and the binding light was exchanged between us.

I caught the light, instead of absorbing it, then siphoned off just a small amount, creating a pendant that looked like a tiny figurine of Owen, and handed it to Cary.

"Present this to Orville. He'll know it's from me. Make sure he knows this is formed from my agreement with your coven that while in my service, while we seek to save Owen, they are safe from you."

He nodded, and from the green shade of his skin, he wasn't relishing the thought of facing the spirits in my home alone, though he'd be with Molly, but she truly was without powers.

"Molly, you must stay in my home until we return. The vipers took you captive, and the moment they realize I exchanged a golem instead of the real Owen, they will seek to take you back. I suspect if they do, they will murder you. The wards on my home and the spirits that dwell there will ensure no one has access to you."

She swallowed hard but nodded. "Okay, go. Cary, once you've spoken with Orville and have Molly safely tucked into our home, you should teleport to Illinois as well. You are a friend of Owen's. Instinctively, I believe that's something that will help him."

Cary nodded, then grabbing Molly's hand, he bobbed his head, and the two disappeared.

"Okay, let's go!" I said, but Mr. Stages stopped me again. He took my hand—something I don't think he did lightly—but held it briefly before he said, "There's no danger as great as when our emotions are involved. We can let those emotions cloud our judgment. You love Owen. I can see and feel that. We all fear that could lead to you becoming entrapped. Balthazar is one of the most dangerous entities on our planet, in our universe. He will seek any weakness to destroy you."

I nodded. "Okay, for this time, I will follow your lead and try to retain my objectivity. I will trust you because Owen is our priority."

He smiled and nodded. "Then we will transport first and manage any traps that've been set."

A light blinked brightly, and instantly, everyone was gone. I waited five seconds, then transported myself. The moment I landed, nothing less than carnage surrounded us. It was a trap, one the witches were all caught in. Those five seconds had saved me from being caught.

I waved my staff and stopped the Balthazar spell from killing the witches, but they were still covered in cuts and bruises. I swept the area with my staff, and probably because my anger was tied to the spell I'd cast, I eradicated all evidence of the magic that'd been here to hurt us.

Balthazar was powerful, but with the light my staff called forth, I was more powerful, and all dark energies needed to be aware of that.

Unfortunately, I hadn't arrived fast enough to save the two witches who'd been slaughtered sometime before. Mr. Stages and the others tended to their corpses.

An older Lincoln was sitting askew in the driveway. Owen had been in there. I could feel him. Something had taken him, though, and the moment I reached the wrecked car, I could feel the vampire. It was hungry. Crap, it was starving, and it craved Owen and the power he represented as the Re'em. All that was clear from the raw emotions that encased the area.

I really would need the witches, and when I turned around, the corpses had been sent somewhere else, and the area had been cleared of blood. The three witches appeared exhausted. Their injuries weren't helping them either.

"Come, let me heal you. We have many battles ahead of us, and I want you as healthy as you can be," I said.

Mr. Stages looked at me strangely. "You have the gift of healing?" he asked.

I nodded. "Yes, and the spirits of your late friends are letting me know they're willing to help you heal."

"Sorcery?" Mrs. Patterson asked aghast.

"No, this isn't sorcery. It's a gift from them to you. Hold still," I said, and wielding my staff, I used the energy from the late witches. Just like Owen's energy had given me strength when I'd created the staff, I healed the injuries of the witches.

I listened as the two spirits told me what to tell the others and laughed before they crossed the veil. "I was told to tell you all that you should, and I quote, 'Kick that vampire's ass.'"

The three witches chuckled, but sadness permeated their reaction. I couldn't heal the sadness. I assumed they'd known these witches, by how they acted. Magic couldn't fix emotions.

That was a good though. All living creatures, magical or not, were meant to feel. It's what made us alive. The ghosts of the witches had also given me another message for their children. I'd keep that one for when the battles had been won and Owen was free.

I could envision the middle-aged witches who'd been the kids of the elderly couple the vampire had murdered. They had both shunned their magical abilities, which is why the couple had been out here doing something they were clearly too old to do. I couldn't fix that any more than I could fix the sadness my witch companions felt, but I sure as hell could avenge their deaths!

CHAPTER FORTY-SIX

OWEN

THINGS WENT FROM BAD to much, much worse. Eric had bitten me twice more before he'd gotten to wherever he was taking me. With each bite, he got stronger, and I got weaker—stupid Eric. And there was absolutely nothing I could do to stop him.

It was pitch-black out, and the clouds covered the moon. I kept thinking I might freeze to death, provided Eric didn't kill me first. I only had so much blood, after all.

Eric had run the entire way from my house to wherever we were now. It, well, it was strange. He was able to run way too quickly for human legs. Almost as fast, if not faster, than a car could drive. How I'd managed to date a fucking vampire that had that ability was beyond me.

I wondered suddenly if he'd been biting me when we dated. Something inside me told me that wasn't the case. If he had, I probably would've been dead, considering Eric got a little crazier every time he bit me.

By the time we arrived and he stopped running, I was exhausted. I doubted I'd even be able to stand. As it turned out, I didn't need to. Eric threw me roughly onto a slab of what felt like rock. It took a moment for my eyes to adjust to the darkness, enough to see there were entities all around me.

"Ah, finally, the Re'em has come," a man, I could barely make out, said. From what I could see, he appeared to be made of stone, tall, and with hard edges to his features. I'd run the other way if I saw him on the street. Hell, I'd run now if I had the energy.

The man leaned over me and sniffed, then turned my head to look at my neck. His hands were so cold it hurt when he touched me. "You!" he yelled at Eric. "You took from him?"

Eric shied away. I couldn't see him in the dark, but I heard him yell as the man attacked him. It was still too dark to make out what happened, but the scream that was abruptly cut off told me Eric didn't survive the attack. I shuddered. Did he just kill Eric right here in front of me?" I hated Eric, but I didn't want him to die.

I tried to move, to get out of there, but I was too weak. Eric had taken too much blood. The man came back and checked me over. Something dark was streaked across his face, and my stomach turned as I realized it must be Eric's blood.

"Get him something for sustenance. The spell won't work if he's this weak. That damned vampire!" he said and walked away. I heard feet scurrying, and a woman, who looked like she couldn't be older than fifteen, came over and lifted me, then waved her hand, and a glass appeared in it.

"This is juice. It'll help you regain your strength."

I thought the man had left, but I heard him barking orders a second after I gulped the orange juice, thankful for it, even if I now knew my life teetered on the edge.

"Get me the Karkadann," he yelled from somewhere to my right.

I was so exhausted, and despite my circumstances, I fell asleep on the cold slab of whatever I was lying on. Dreams of dark shadows played around me. I could barely move, but when I did, my body felt too big and lethargic, different from my normal self.

I flicked a glance down at my feet and realized, maybe, just maybe, Eric hadn't been wrong in showing me the image of a unicorn, but how the hell was that possible? How, if I was, had the witches and Damian not known?"

In the dream, I could see much better than when I was awake. The dark creatures around me were menacing, to say the least, and I could see the man now. He was exactly as I'd seen him in the dark earlier. He was like a walking statue. His skin was intensely pale and almost transparent. I glanced toward where I'd heard Eric scream, and even though he wasn't there, a pool of blood marked the spot. I seriously doubted he'd survived.

I could hear words, and although it was like listening through water, I knew the creepy, murdering man had begun to chant. Then, magically, a group of people appeared in front of him. Shadow, Molly's friend, appeared with them.

She immediately turned toward me, and concern flickered across her face before she schooled her expression and looked toward the man.

I focused until their words became clearer. "We must perform the spell before the morning breaks. It's just luck the stupid vampire stumbled on the Re'em on the new moon."

He turned toward where I lay and shook his head. "It's not ideal that he's lost so much blood. He should be fitter to undergo the transformation, but needs must. I won't have that wizard interfering again."

I knew he meant Damian, and hope sprang up inside me. The creepy man was afraid of Damian.

"What should we do with the golem?" one of the men who'd appeared with Shadow asked the statue guy.

"Aah, that could be useful. Bring him to me."

Just then, my human form appeared in front of the statue man. I watched as my doppelganger struggled against the arms that held him, and then he froze when he saw me. "Please, let me go. Please," he said.

The statue man lifted his hand, and I watched in shock as it turned into a massive knifelike thing. Then, without hesitation, he decapitated...well...me. He decapitated me!

I sucked in a breath, causing the statue man to turn toward me. "Aah, you have regained some of your strength. Good, that's very good," he said.

He turned away from me, reached down, and pulled a parchment out of the mouth of the thing that had been me but was now just a pile of clay. This was the weirdest dream I'd ever had.

The statue guy took the paper and smelled it. "Yes, this is perfect, the blood of the wizard!"

He squeezed the paper, and I watched, terrified, as blood dripped from it into a vial that magically appeared in the statue guy's hand.

"Dungun," he called, and a creepy, dark antlike creature came over. "Get the witches to bind the blood to my dagger," he said, handing over the vial and a huge knife he'd pulled out of a holster on his side.

"Now, Karkadann, you can embed your little Re'em friend here with some energy, can you not? We need him ready for the spell that comes."

Shadow nodded, and it appeared as if she smiled slightly. She came toward me, transforming as she did into some bizarre antelope thing with black scales. She looked more like a dragon but for the long, inky black horn that protruded from her head.

The moment she got to where I was lying, she lowered the horn and stuck me in the belly. I felt the pain first, then warmth flowed into me. With it, I heard the words, "Don't worry, I'm on your side, but don't let anyone know!"

She pulled back, and even in my dream state, the world went dark.

CHAPTER FORTY-SEVEN

DAMIAN

T HE TRAIL WAS HIDDEN from us, which was utterly frustrating. How could that stupid vampire hide his trail from me?

We wandered around the yard until Cary showed up. Frustrated, I finally remembered my phone had buzzed earlier. I pulled it out of my pocket and opened it to see the message was from Owen. My heart contracted.

"We have to find him," I said, fear overcoming me.

The four witches looked at me sadly. Cary placed his hand on my shoulder. "Try not to let Owen's kidnapping get to you too much. We need you to stay focused, okay?" he asked, but nothing anyone said could make me less anxious about losing Owen.

Mr. Stages had been right. I was in love with him and wanted him back so I could protect him and love him for the rest of our lives.

Cary froze as something appeared behind me. "Um, I think that's for you," he said and nodded in that direction.

I turned and saw a very wary ghost standing just a few feet away. "Tell them not to approach, or I will leave!" the young woman said.

"If you're here to help, they won't harm you. They've taken an oath."

That seemed to mollify the ghost enough that she approached me. "The spirits from here to Seattle are working together to find your guy. We think we know where he is," she said, giving me hope for the first time since we found the car.

"Where? Show us!" I demanded, and she put her hand on mine.

"Follow me," she said and disappeared. I could still feel her though. When she'd touched me, she'd imprinted on me how to sense her, something I didn't know ghosts could do.

I nodded at the witches beside me and, using my staff, cast the spell to pull all of us behind the ghost. I could feel the witches' skepticism, but I couldn't help but think that was their prejudice weighing in. I had no reason not to trust the ghost, especially if she'd come to me with witches, her most ardent enemy, to help us find Owen.

When we landed at the site of an old house, which was basically a hole with mud walls and a roof that had long ago collapsed, another spirit of an ancient old man stared out into the distance. "They're up to no good out there," he said, turning toward me.

He sized up the witches and sighed. "No need to push me through that confounded veil. I'm willing to go on my own."

"Not tonight, you don't have to. The witches have vowed not to bother anyone in my service who helps me tonight to save my boyfriend. You qualify as that, sir."

"Boyfriend, you say? As in a man?" he asked, and I cringed, ready to hear a lecture about homosexuality. I nodded, though, and the old man smiled. "So nice things have changed. In my day, I couldn't have a boyfriend or even admit I had one. I suspect that's why I'm still here, still searching for a way to reconcile all I lost in that time."

I smiled at the old man and would've liked to console him, but there was still too much at stake. "Thank you. I am forever in your debt."

"Go get your man. I'll stay here and watch. Whatever's out there has created a boundary not even I can get past."

I nodded, then looked at my witch friends. "How do you propose we proceed?" I asked.

"Carefully," Mr. Harrison replied instantly.

The wave of darkness hit us, and I knew we'd already been detected. "Brace for it!" I said just as the second wave hit. This time, fully intending to cause us harm.

My staff was already in my hand, and I shielded us from the worst of the blast. The four witches surrounded me then, each taking a spot in a formation very much like the four points of a compass: north, south, east, west. That's all I needed to know to understand what they wanted from me.

I drew my power from them as they drew it in from each direction. Mr. Stages stood to the north, and the energy that flowed through him and into the staff was powerful. Mr. Harrison stood to the south, and it, too, was powerful enough to fight any enemy we might face.

East and West held their powers, as well. Cary was holding the western flank. The energy grew the longer we stood, and nothing the dark sent at us was remotely strong enough to intercede until a magical arrow pierced through the protections and slammed into me.

I flew into the air and froze. I recognized Balthazar as he rode the air toward us, a malicious smile smeared across his face.

I could barely move, unsure how he had bested me. The Legacy Wizard was supposed to be stronger than any dark force, except my own dark equivalent. That entity was an immortal buried deep within the earth below a mountain in Norway. Balthazar was not him.

From my peripheral vision, I saw all four of the witches were each encased in some kind of bubble. They all writhed in pain, and I fought to get free to, if nothing else, save them.

"Aah, you've come to watch my party," Balthazar said as he entered our circle. "How nice of you. Oh, and how nice of you to provide your own blood to ensure you couldn't intervene. I would stop resisting if I were you. You donated enough of your DNA to keep you trapped for at least another twenty-four hours."

At first, I had no idea how he'd gotten my blood, but then—the golem! I'd forgotten I'd put a golem into the hands of the vipers. The only way to give a golem life was with the creator's blood. Damn, had I just sealed Owen's fate?

Balthazar couldn't kill me. Intuitively, I knew my powers would prevent that. He could, however, kill Owen and the witches while I watched. With his blood spell, there was not a damned thing I could do to stop him.

Balthazar waved a wand that magically appeared in his hand, and we all floated behind him. When we got to a spot surrounded by what appeared to be thorny bushes and locust trees, I saw a real unicorn lying on a slab. It was some sort of altar, and although I couldn't ascertain what kind of magic they did there, another symptom of being held in the blood spell, I sensed it was deeply embedded in the dark.

"Karkadann, it's time!" Balthazar said, and I watched as Shadow, the woman who'd pretended to be my friend, the one who'd gotten Molly mixed up in all this crap, wandered into view, a look of pure arrogance on her face.

"Do it, dark witches. Start the chants!"

I heard a low hum like a thousand voices making the same note, and then dark witches came forward, each dressed in dark clothing. Some seemed way too old to be alive. I knew dark witches could prolong their lives, but not without doing serious damage to their souls. These were no longer healthy witches, and their humming drew from an energy outside this world.

Demonic would be the word a layperson would call this energy. I knew it was more than that. It was a bastardization of the very darkness they served. Dark didn't want destruction. It wanted balance. I felt that the instant the nasty aura came into my presence. If I'm right, and I pray to the gods that I am, dark would resist. I didn't know how, but I was happy to feel awareness that it would.

Would it be enough to save Owen? I had no idea, but I hoped beyond hope.

Shadow shifted from her human shape into the Karkadann. In any other situation, I would say the creature was as beautiful in its darkness as Owen was in his Re'em state. It was then that it struck me: the Karkadann was not the enemy of the Re'em. Could it be? Was Shadow Owen's salvation? I dared not even have that much hope.

I watched as the power grew around us. Inky, unnatural darkness swirling in dark foglike rings. It smelled of death and decay but also sulfur. What were the words used in old times? Oh, brimstone. It smelled of death and brimstone.

Shadow, in Karkadann form, moved forward slowly, and I realized she was waiting for something. There were thousands of creatures around us. Maybe even hundreds of thousands. As each creature lifted its voice along with the dark witches, I noticed a dark glow, literally dark energy growing around Balthazar. It was then I realized what his end goal was.

"You're trying to absorb the Re'em's energy?" I asked, hoping to distract him, to distract them.

A wave of dark energy hit me so hard I felt nauseous, but with it came Balthazar's response. "The era of the Re'em is over. No more will it reincarnate. After tonight, the darkness will remain in power forever."

I strained against my restraints. I couldn't let that happen. I had to stop it somehow, some way. Yet, I couldn't undo a curse that used my own blood against me. Fuck, how had I let this happen?

When all the entities' voices joined together, the sound made me feel as if it could pull my soul from my body. It was both loud and too quiet at the same time. It was so unnatural, so out of, well, out of balance. It was the opposite of me and everything I stood for.

Balthazar yelled then, "Now, Karkadann, do it now!"

Shadow, in her Karkadann form, rose on two legs. The dark energy that flowed around Balthazar glowed on the tip of her horn. She faced Owen, who lay unconscious on the slab. I screamed as she came down, her horn pointing directly at my beloved Owen. Tonight, the world as we knew it was going to end, and with it was going to be the death of the only man, the only creature I would ever love.

Chapter Forty-Eight

OWEN

I woke as a hum began to echo around me. I almost got up, but I heard Shadow in my head. *"Don't move, not until I tell you to. You and I must join to stop this."*

I knew, somehow, she told the truth. Shadow was my only salvation. I almost lost my shit, though, when I looked up and saw all four of my witch friends encased in bubbles and Damian somehow locked into a spell I sensed he couldn't get out of.

"Stay calm. They're okay. Trust me, Owen!" Shadow said in my mind.

"Okay, but hurry."

"They all must sing. I have to wait, patience. Trust me," she said again.

I watched as she moved slowly toward me, glancing from her to my friends, and I managed to keep myself from moving, from giving away any plans to the statue creep, who was now somehow glowing darkly.

When the sound reached a horrifying pitch, Shadow, in her weird, whatever she was, form, lifted on her hind legs. Fear gripped me before she screamed, "Now!"

Instinct took over, and I jumped from the slab and turned toward her just as her horn came down. My horn and hers collided, and a strange rainbow-colored supernova burst from where our two horns met.

Power soared through me, and strength like I'd never known settled firmly into my being. The horrific hum ceased, and moments later, the light slowly ebbed, and Shadow pulled back. The second after she did, we both turned back into what I now knew were human avatars—the human equivalent of our bodies.

"We did it, brother."

"Brother?" I asked, and I knew what she was saying was true. Shadow was my sister.

I looked over at where the dark entities had been, but only ashes wafted through the air now. "Incinerated?" I asked, and Shadow nodded.

"Destroyed themselves by linking to my horn when you and I joined. Not a smart move."

"Wait!" I yelled. "Damian, Cary!"

"They're fine. Come on. They're over here."

I followed her as we rushed to where all five lay crumpled on the ground. I could feel that Mrs. Patterson was injured, but the moment Shadow saw her, she turned back into the

Karkadann and touched her with her horn. Mrs. Patterson's injuries were immediately healed.

She swallowed hard as she gazed up at Shadow and whispered, "Thanks."

Shadow transformed back into her human avatar and smiled, then reached down and pulled Mrs. Patterson to her feet.

I rushed over to Damian and pulled him up. Seeing he was okay and smiling at me, I thrust myself into his arms. "Oh my God, Damian, I was so worried," I cried, tears pouring down my face.

"Shh, my powerful unicorn, you were magnificent, as was Shadow. Thank you," he said over my shoulder.

"Ah, nothing to it," she said.

I didn't have the energy to unpack how it was nothing.

Damian held me tight, whispering it was okay and that it was over. Finally, after a very long time, I let him go. The tears finally spent.

"You're fine, and I dare say, nothing in its right mind will ever take you on again. You are a fully powered unicorn, after all."

I shook my head. "I have no idea what that means, but if I don't have to worry about being abducted again or bitten by a stupid vampire, I am fully behind it."

"Yeah, we'll still need to check on the bites."

"No, you don't," Shadow said. "He's pure light, remember. Nothing can infect him now, not when he and I have completed our joining."

"About that," Damian said, but Shadow laughed.

"About that, you can never say what you saw here today. In fact, I either get your commitment in blood, or I will erase all your memories, and I do mean all of them," she said.

Somehow, I knew she...we...actually could do just that. Even a Legacy Wizard couldn't resist the combined powers of Re'em and Karkadann unicorns.

Damian smiled at me. "I would never do anything to hurt Owen or the future reincarnations of him either," he said, and I couldn't help but smile even though the thought of being reincarnated opened up so many questions.

Shadow looked around the group, and when they all agreed, she transformed and touched each of their hands with her horn, releasing a small amount of blood.

"Swear," she said as she returned to her avatar form, "that you will never speak of what you saw here tonight. No one must ever know the unified power of the Re'em or Karkadann unicorns."

They all swore simultaneously, and dark rainbow light glowed in their hands, sealing their promises.

Satisfied, Shadow sighed. "Now, if you give Owen and me a moment, we need to speak, and since I've claimed this as my territory, there is no place safer for us to do so."

I could tell Damian didn't want to leave me, not again, and not so soon after my life had been in jeopardy, but when I nodded in his direction, he went with the others.

"So," I said as soon as they were gone, "want to explain what happened?"

"Yes, but only in our natural form. You will understand it much better that way."

I didn't need to think. I transformed just as Shadow did. The sun crested the horizon as Shadow sent images of her life as a young child.

Our father, the son of a bitch, had fathered her with another woman while married to my mother. I had been conceived one day later. Shadow and I were born on the same night, just seconds apart. Of course, Shadow had been born first.

"In most of our past lives, we've been twins, but you were destroyed in the last three reincarnations, so I assume that's why the gods must've given us two different mothers."

"And our dad?" I asked in my head, using words instead of images.

"Total asshole. Best to avoid him, but our grandmother is pretty awesome," she responded.

She showed me images of our father's parents and how they had loved her. They were from a long line of magical beings, not quite witches, although that's who they usually married or hung out with.

Our father's mother had suspected Shadow was different, and when our grandfather passed, she began to test Shadow's gifts, pulling the Karkadann to the forefront earlier than it might've occurred naturally.

Luckily for me, that's what'd happened, otherwise, she wouldn't have been knowledgeable enough to save us from Balthazar.

We galloped along the prairie through empty corn fields and over a multitude of fences when, finally, I transformed into my human avatar and sat down on the porch at a vacant house. Shadow transformed as well and sat next to me.

"Can I visit her?" I asked, meaning our grandmother. I hadn't known my mother's mom. But I'd loved my grandfather with everything I had in me. He was more of a dad if I was being honest. Mom was annoying, but I knew she'd always loved me, unlike my dad, who had disappeared long ago.

"She's very frail, but she'd love to meet you. I-I think she always wondered about you. Re'em are always male, and Karkadann always female. Grandma would've known you existed."

"Why didn't she try to find me?" I asked, feeling a bit put out by that new information.

Shadow leaned back against the old rotted post and sighed. "Listen, the dark never attacks Karkadann. For one thing, even the legends tell of how territorial we are." She chuckled, but I think even I knew how powerful she was.

"When the Re'em is young, they are completely without powers. Even with my protection, you would've been in jeopardy. Grandma couldn't risk the forces that attacked you tonight finding you until you were ready."

"Ready? How is it I was ready? I mean, I still don't believe it, and I literally just changed back into a human."

Shadow laughed. "Yeah, it's going to take time. I've had an entire lifetime, and it still sometimes shocks me."

I shook my head as Shadow continued.

"Listen, I have no idea how it works for the Re'em. I had my powers from the moment I was born. They've just become more powerful as I've grown older. I suspect when you moved to Seattle, and yes, before you ask, I've done a lot of research on you since we met that night in my bar."

"Your bar?" I asked, causing her to chuckle.

"My bar. I own it, and several other establishments in Seattle."

"Wait. There's some bad juju there, Damian told me..."

"Yeah, and they are all dead now. Listen, there's so much to unpack about what happened tonight, what's been happening. Balthazar confronted me after I went out with the leader of the stupid vipers. He threatened Molly if I didn't help him find my light equivalent, in other words, you. At first, he didn't believe me when I told him I didn't know you. I wasn't powerful enough, not until we were joined, to defeat him, but I bided my time. Unfortunately, the son of a bitch was there that night you came in. He recognized you before I did. I thought maybe I could hire you as my attorney, then... it didn't work out as I'd hoped. When I refused to help him kill you, he kidnapped Molly, and I had to come up with a strategy to defeat him. All I can say is, luckily, Damian stepped in when he did with that ridiculous golem and got her released from Balthazar's grip."

"Wait—the golem. That's what got him in so much trouble?"

Shadow smiled sadly. "Yeah, it's a Hebrew thing. It's a clay figure you can bring to life. Unfortunately, I didn't even think about him using his own blood." She shook her head. "If Balthazar wasn't the exhibitionist he was, he could've done a lot more damage with that than just holding him and your witch friends captive."

Images rolled through my mind of how Damian's blood could've been honed into a weapon to use against the light. "Yeah," I said as the images began to subside. "He'd best keep his blood to himself from now on."

Shadow chuckled beside me.

I thought about Molly, and it hit me like a ton of bricks. "Wait, you...you and Molly?" I asked.

Shadow sighed. "You're coming into your powers. That's going to be a bit disconcerting, especially since they'll be coming on you fast now. You'll want to find somewhere you can lie low. Of course, you're welcome to stay here. Nothing would dare come into the Karkadann territory, not even humans, although they wouldn't understand why not."

I chuckled. "I have a feeling I'll be safe with Damian."

"For sure, but if you ever need a place, as my brother and my opposite, you are welcome here anytime."

"Back to Molly," I said, causing Shadow to laugh.

"Yes, I've been in love with her for a while, but that's probably done now. She thinks I set her up with Balthazar. I had to play along with him, or he would've killed her. I couldn't let him do that, even if she hates me forever."

The sun was shining now. I felt my internal power rise and couldn't help but chuckle. "I am some sort of love charm, aren't I?" I asked, knowing the answer was yes.

Shadow laughed. "Love is a pure light emotion, and even when it comes from a dark source, you'll sense it."

"Molly doesn't hate you. She's confused. I can feel her emotions even here. You would be wise to talk to her sooner rather than later though. Wow, eew, I shouldn't be able to feel all those emotions, especially if you're my sister, yuck!"

Shadow burst into laughter as I shut down all the insight regarding how much the two women liked and, well, loved each other. They had a pretty good sex life. Yuck! I chuckled, this time at my own reaction.

"Let's get back to Seattle. I'll talk to her."

"Wait, can you... I, um, this is your territory, right? I feel like that's a big deal."

Shadow nodded. "Let your intuition guide you, look deeper," she suggested, and when I did, I could see it. The Karkadann territory was significant for a variety of reasons. Eventually, she would raise her children here, children who would be the forebearers of our reincarnated selves. Until then, she could travel anywhere there was dark.

I could travel anywhere there is light. Together, we could travel anywhere, period. That included a lot of outer space options, although I couldn't quite make out what that meant yet. I certainly would, though, as time went on.

"Come on. Your wizard is about to crack. You know, I might not have your abilities to sense love, but I can certainly feel how much he loves you."

"Please, we just met; we barely know each other."

Shadow stopped me right before I transformed, which was required if we were going to travel. "You've known him many lifetimes. He's a reincarnated wizard, just as you are a reincarnated Re'em. You may have never been lovers, although I suspect you were, but your bond is deeper than one incarnation. Don't resist how you feel for him. Time in each life is short and precious. It will be gone quickly enough, and you must hold onto it while you can."

I nodded, her words striking true even as she spoke.

"Okay, and the same goes for you and Molly. I sense something deep. Much deeper than this lifetime, as well."

Shadow smiled and hugged me. "Okay, I am ready to go home. Shall we?"

I stopped. "Ugh, no. Damn, I forgot my mom's dog. I have to take her out."

"Okay, we'll stop there first and then home!" she said.

I realized with the sun up, she depended on me to initiate the travel, but I didn't laugh. I felt her need to see Molly and wanted to see my own man.

Luckily, as we arrived outside my mom's place, she came out of the house and asked where I'd been, then turned to Shadow, her eyebrow arched.

"Mom," I said with a sigh. "Shit, I might as well tell you what I know."

We spent the next hour talking to Mom about how Dad had another kid, and Shadow was my half-sister.

Mom cried a little, and both of us consoled her. "I knew," Mom said. "I don't know how I knew, but I did. Anyway, I'm glad you found each other. Maybe now I can let that man go. Oh, Eric, I need to fix that."

I opened my mouth to tell her Eric was gone, but Shadow shook her head, reached over, and laid her hand on my mother's back. Dark light flowed into Mom, and I knew all memory of Eric was disappearing.

I joined my hand over hers and replaced the memories of Eric with positive ones, and together, Shadow and I called upon someone who could take Eric's place as Mom's law partner. Someone who would be a good replacement.

Dark replaces dark, though, and I knew Shadow was calling on a dark witch to take his place. If he was under Shadow's influence, he'd be a good guy or woman...yes, that felt more right. Eric's replacement would be a woman. Mom would like that.

When the power subsided, Mom seemed tired. "Well, kids, it's been so nice to see you, but all this traveling has made me tired," she said and walked upstairs to her bedroom.

"She won't even remember we came, will she?" I asked.

Shadow smiled but shook her head. "Nope, so you better grab your things so as not to confuse her."

"Cool," I said, and after collecting all my luggage, which was luckily still packed, we transformed, touched horns, and just like that, we were in Damian's front yard, my luggage sitting next to us. Correction, our front yard, I was home, and Damian was my beloved partner. It was time for me to accept that and stop running away.

CHAPTER FORTY-NINE

DAMIAN

EXHAUSTED, WE TELEPORTED BACK to the cemetery before the sun rose, thus keeping ourselves hidden from nonmagical and magical eyes alike.

I took a moment to fill Mr. Stages in on what the ghosts of his friends had told me to relay to their kids before I went home. He assured me he'd give them the message.

I had a feeling now that Shadow had claimed that part of Illinois as her territory, the witches around her would be a bit more active. The Karkadann was a powerful creature known to create a lot of energy around her.

If my intuition was telling me correctly, the Arabic culture had spent copious amounts of time describing her and her power. Mostly they were scared shitless of her, as was wise. Very wise.

I missed Owen. All that'd gone down, all the mistakes I'd made almost destroyed him. I was almost sure Shadow was telling him to leave me the fuck alone, run and never look back. I got home to a very upset household.

"What? What's happening?" I asked Orville when I walked in and he and several of the other ghosts rushed me at the door,

"Is...is he okay?" Orville asked, and I knew he meant Owen.

"Yeah, he's good. Just spending time with his sister."

Relief washed over him, and he came in for a hug. I did the spell fast enough that when he collided with me, he was physically able to hug me. Of course, the moment he pulled away, he transformed back into a spirit.

"Oh, the ghosts, our sources from Illinois, said... They said horrible things."

I nodded. "It was horrible, Orville," I said as the other ghosts stood silently listening. "I will tell you all the details later, but yes, I sorta screwed up, but Shadow, my friend? The one that came with Molly the first time? She saved him and all of us."

Magically, I was reminded of my agreement to not disclose who she and Owen were, and stopped before I said more. "Where's Molly?" I asked to distract from the abrupt end of my conversation.

"She's here," Alice said from the parlor. The door was closed, but Alice came through it and over to me. "She was so afraid, but about an hour ago, she said, 'They're fine,' then fell asleep."

I smiled. Somehow, Molly had sensed the end of it all. I wasn't surprised, even as a nonmagical. Shadow and I were her besties, not to mention her new friends Owen and Cary. She was probably linked to all of us, and all of us being magical, naturally, she would've felt something.

I opened the pocket door, walked to where Molly lay, and kissed her forehead. She moaned a bit and rolled over, so I pulled the throw I assumed Alice had laid over her up, so it covered her better. It was cold, so I also flicked my hand, making a small fire in the fireplace, and smiling when I realized one of the ghosts must've cleaned out the flue and replaced the logs after we'd last used it.

I closed the door behind me and went up to the attic. I wouldn't be able to sleep until Owen got home, but I was still in pain from when the blood spell had bound me. I needed rest, even if it wasn't accompanied by sleep.

"Orville, tell me if Molly wakes or Shadow and Owen get home," I said, remembering I'd blocked Orville from the attic. I quickly brought forth my staff and severed the bindings that kept him out, no longer having any internal strength to do it myself.

Even a small spell was too much for my body.

I stripped my clothes off and climbed into the shower. Blood magic had a distinct smell, and I was covered with it, which was making me nauseous. And even as tired as I was, I didn't want to get in bed until that smell was gone.

By the time I got out of the shower, the sun was up, making me feel a little better. Owen was sending me positive energy, and that was enough so when I lay down and closed my eyes, I fell into a blissful sleep. My thoughts filled with Owen, a beautiful and powerful magical beast I loved with my entire soul.

Chapter Fifty

OWEN

I SMILED WHEN WE showed up inside the house. Had it been anyone but Shadow and me, Damian's and Elias's wards would've stopped them dead. I doubt even the hateful Balthazar could've penetrated them.

I felt Molly in the parlor, and sure enough, when I opened the door, she was sleeping on the sofa. "I'll leave you to it," I said, knowing Shadow needed to handle that without me. I rushed up the stairs and almost collided with a very concerned-looking Orville. "Mr. Lloyd, we've been so worried," he said before I could dash up the stairs and into Damian's arms.

I reached out and touched Orville, and where my hand landed, he became solid, like I'd seen when Damian had cast a spell to make it so they could connect with the living.

Orville gasped, and I smiled. "I've got a few secrets up my sleeve too," I said, leaving the secret to be just that. It would be better if the ghosts in my care understood I'd become something different. Even with my powers as strong as they were, all unicorn species understood we needed to keep our identity a secret.

I wasn't vulnerable, at least not now, but that didn't mean we wouldn't be when we reincarnated again. My link with the Legacy Wizard could end up harming my future incarnations. Connections are dangerous, as was demonstrated by the nasty Balthazar and the other dark entities who'd supported him.

Once Orville and the other ghosts were soothed, I rushed up the stairs and into my beloved Damian's arms. I jumped on him, waking him up. He woke laughing, and I didn't hesitate to take his mouth with mine.

"I love you," I admitted when I pulled back.

He studied me for a moment and then smiled. "It's so much more than love that I feel for you. I don't even have the words, Owen. I'm completely and utterly devoted to you."

"Mmm," I said, "Could be worse things than having a Legacy Wizard devoted to you, huh?"

He smiled and kissed me. "Could be worse things than having the one and only Re'em unicorn loving you, huh?"

"Truth," I said and ground my cock into him. "I say we should celebrate our good fortune."

Before I knew it, Damian had magically flipped me onto my back. "I couldn't agree with you more!"

We made passionate love for the rest of the afternoon. Then, we slept in each other's arms until the following morning.

Both of us were utterly exhausted from the previous day's encounters.

Dreams for me were different now—more like visions. I was awake but not. Something I guess came with being the Re'em. I saw when Molly and Shadow left the house. Shadow stopped just before leaving, turned toward me, and winked, letting me know she could see me. I also think she and Molly had made up.

The vision of her and Molly living in Illinois, where Shadow and I had sat this morning as their main home, filled me with joy. Then, the vision of three little ones, two girls and a boy running through the wild fields, caused me nothing less than happiness.

EPILOGUE: OWEN

"D O WIZARDS AND UNICORNS need to get married?" I asked, frustrated with all the hoopla Cary was tossing at me.

"Yes, they do, and you shouldn't be announcing you're a unicorn."

"I blocked the office when I came back to work. Jeez, I'm the freaking Re'em. I know basic shit," I said, causing Cary to chuckle.

I'd been antsy since Damian had proposed in a grand, spectacular way. We were in the Mt. Pleasant graveyard, the only place where the ghosts felt comfortable being with the witches, even though Damian had brokered a peace agreement between them over a year earlier.

We wanted to have a party with all our friends, but the ghosts still refused to let the witches into our home, saying it put the wards at risk, which, ironically, the witches had said as well. The compromise was when we wanted a party, we had it at the cemetery and at night when we could have privacy.

Our lives certainly were strange. Damian had surprised me, which as a unicorn, is freaking hard to do. I knew he had done something with Shadow to keep it a secret—something I'd given her a shit ton of grief about afterward.

Our sweet grandmother had passed away just a week after I'd met her. She smiled at me when I met her and said she'd waited for me, and I couldn't have been happier that at least before she'd passed on, I'd had the opportunity.

Since then, Shadow and I had grown closer. Shadow was, in every way, an environmentalist. I didn't know until our grandmother told me that she'd finished her Ph.D. in Environmental Studies. All her music was about saving the Earth.

Now that the dark forces were so determined to create an imbalance, our focus, both Shadow's and mine, had been on reversing the darkness created by humanity. Not all things dark came from the magical community.

If we didn't reverse the climate change and other horrors created by fossil fuels and polluting the oceans, there would be a much greater risk of destroying the balance of life on earth than anything Balthazar had tried to create. Luckily, my being an attorney and Shadow, an influential performer, we had significant impacts, even if they were subtle.

Life was busy as we all took to our duties. That didn't mean we weren't a close-knit family. Even the ghosts allowed Cary to visit now without getting pissy about it. On top of that, Cary introduced Cook, also known as Lucious, to some ghost they'd met on the Illinois prairie, and the two had hit it off.

Now, Lucious adored Cary, although he was still leery of him. Alexander, the old man ghost who allowed himself to revert to a younger version when he met Lucious, now lived together in our armory, next to the kitchen.

I'd never been in the room and hadn't even remembered it was there until I got home and felt it with my Re'em senses. Luckily, now that the worst of the dark forces that threatened us had disintegrated in their attack against me, there wasn't much need for weapons.

So, Damian had created a strange sort of dimensional pocket where the weapons were stored in case we needed them, freeing the armory for the two ghost lovers to have their own privacy. Which, at least to me, was entirely appropriate.

I allowed Cary, and now his accomplice, Mrs. Patterson, to dress me in what seemed like an outfit better suited for a freaking cosplay event at some con.

As I stared at myself in the mirror, the bright white, wildly out-of-date tuxedo looked pretty sweet on me. Begrudgingly, I admitted that.

The wedding was quite an event, but I refused to have my fucking wedding in a graveyard, so we rented a downtown cathedral, where luckily, the priest was a witch and a friend of Mr. Stages. The witches agreed to leave our ghost friends alone, so they, too, could attend. I think having both Shadow and me being rather insistent about that helped persuade them.

Shadow and Molly had refused to let Damian and me see each other before the event. It felt weird they were both so committed to a conventional wedding, considering theirs had been in the middle of an Iraqi desert, where Shadow had told us all that every Karkadann wedding had been held since the beginning of time.

As her brother and the Re'em, I knew that was total bullshit, but I didn't contradict her. It was a beautiful ceremony, convened by a powerful djinn, who I suspected was the real reason Shadow had wanted to get married there.

In the form of elephants, djinn had been the bane of Karkadanns existence throughout history, and now that the dark forces that plagued her were dealt with, I suspected Shadow wanted to play nice with the djinn to avoid any chaos their millennia-old feud might cause.

Regardless, here I was at my enormous wedding, with magical creatures on both the dark and light side, sitting in an enormous cathedral, with a powerful witch presiding. My life was so much it was hard to put words to how I felt.

Cary and Mrs. Patterson brushed down my tux as Mom wept and told me how handsome I was. Poor Mom had no clue so many powerful magical creatures surrounded her. Not that her status as a powerful human diminished her in any way. Mom was a force to be reckoned with, no matter what circles she ran in.

The moment I spotted Damian, I realized all we'd been through, the wizard, witches, abduction, vampire bites... all that'd happened had been worth it.

Damian's tux was similar to mine in style but dark blue. He was so handsome, and the tux accented his features perfectly. Dammit, Cary knew what he was doing.

Tears leaked from my eyes as Damien took my hand, and we walked down the aisle toward the altar. I froze for a moment. I'd thought Mr. Stages would perform the ceremony, but instead, the man who'd read my cards on the plane stood there. Mr. Stages stood next to Mrs. Patterson and Cary.

Damian had spotted him too and, in his telepathic way, told me he was the man who'd given him the wizard ring—the one who'd started the whole wizard quest.

It seemed appropriate that he was the officiant, considering he'd been the one to set us both on our combined life journeys. Apparently, he was going to make our life together official.

Rainbows danced around us, dark and light, as the crowd threw their magic toward us, gracing our union with their delight.

The moment we stopped in front of the altar, silence filled the cathedral, and it was just Damian and me in front of the strange card reader. Cary, Mr. Stages, and Mrs. Patterson stood to my side while Molly, Shadow, and Orville stood to his. Mr. Harrison held my mother's hand in the front row behind us.

"Do you take this wizard as your lawfully and magically wedded husband?" he asked me, and happy tears rolled from my eyes.

"From now until the end of eternity," I said, and a light lifted from my heart and hung above our heads.

Without glancing up, the officiant asked Damian the same thing, but this time, instead of wizard, he asked if he would take me, the magical creature I was, as his lawfully and magically wedded husband.

Damian squeezed my hand, and when he agreed, a bluish light came out of his chest and combined with mine.

We looked up as the lights entwined and then separated, blue and white, as they flowed onto our hands, forming identical bands.

"With these magical rings," the officiant said, his smile growing even wider, "I declare you mated in this life and beyond."

I kissed Damian as my heart filled with so much love for him I thought it might burst. We turned, the spell that'd encircled us fell, and we could hear the cheers filling the vast space.

I glanced at Mom, who appeared perplexed but happy. My intuition hit me hard as I realized there was more than just friendship between my mom and Mr. Harrison, but now wasn't the time to worry about my mother and boss's relationship. Today was about my new husband and mate.

Today was about the beauty of love and the power of happiness that a love like ours brought with it.

WHAT'S NEXT?

books2read.com/NoJusticefortheDamned

No rest for the wicked. No justice for the damned.

New Mason City is home to the damned, the depraved, the most wicked of all sinners. Killian is no different. Assassin, prostitute, brother and son; he's proven himself to be obedient and deadly when it comes to carrying out the orders of the man who raised him: the priest called Father.

Killian's life is simple. Reliable. It consists of serving Father without fail, ensuring the compliance of the players in Father's drug trafficking ring, and doing everything in his power to preserve his straining relationship with his adopted brother, Abraham.

But a perhaps less than chance encounter with a mysterious man called Hollow, calls into question everything Killian has ever believed. New memories of a childhood he can barely recall come to the surface, forcing him to question what's true and what's been planted in his mind by something stranger than fiction...magic.

Now, thrust into a frightening new reality, Killian must determine who to trust: the man who raised him, protected him, cared for him. Or the man who's begun to haunt his dreams and fill his mind with visions of a past that terrifies him. Who claims to know the depths of his very soul.

When all parties are damned, can there truly be any justice?

TALES FROM THE TAROT

Grab the 22-book series at mybook.to/talesfromthetarot

Found in Obscurity by A.M. Rose

Twisted Fates by Adam J. Ridley

No Justice for the Damned by Hellie Heat

The Angel's Kiss by Nicholas Bella

Death Song by B. Ripley

Arcanum by Ashlyn Drewek

The Devil's Dilemma by Alex J. Adams

Camelot's Tower by Brooke Matthews

A Highland Gargoyle's Lucky Star by Chloe Archer

Trust in the Moon by Delaney Rain

Raising the Sun by Eryn Hawk

Zero Judgment by Kota Quinn

The End of the World by Drake LaMarque

ABOUT THE AUTHOR

After years of writing romance under the pen name Blake Allwood, I decided to pursue my other genre passion, fantasy and science fiction. Adam J. Ridley is the reality of that pursuit.

My husband of 28 years and I have had an adventurous life. We've had many businesses, we've raised over twelve foster children, two of which we adopted, and had at least two professional careers.

To say we are people who seek experiences is an understatement.

As I've grown older, my passions seem to be better reflected in my imagination. Fantasy, urban fantasy, and science fiction all allow me to escape into worlds that transcend life. I've always been a major lover of fantasy writing and started reading it at a rather young age.

My husband and I travel full-time now in our RV (caravan for those not in the United States.) We've been doing this since 2017 and y'all, we love it.

Please join me on Facebook, and other social media sites. I work hard to be easily accessible to my readers, cause you all are the reason for all the lovely work!

ALSO BY
ADAM J. RIDLEY

The Witch Brothers Saga
Fantasy

Big Bend Series
Paranormal Romantic Suspense

Emergence
A Superhero Novel

...and more at adamjridley.com